The fighter had a dream. . . .

*Some men were sewing a body into canvas.
It was on the deck of a ship. There was a
big seam up the middle of the canvas, and
now only the face was still uncovered . . .*

*"You want to take a last look, champ?" one
of the men asked. "We're about ready to
dump him."*

*The fighter bent to see in the moonlight.
The face in the canvas was his own . . .*

The fighter was Luke Pilgrim, middleweight
champion of the world. Luke could handle any
man in the ring. He also could handle the hoods
who were trying to muscle in on his next fight . . .
But there was one thing he couldn't handle —
and that was murder . . .

"That great rarity, a good sports mystery..."
— The New York Times

WILLIAM CAMPBELL GAULT

Author of:
The Bloody Bokhara
Don't Cry For Me

The Canvas Coffin

William Campbell Gault

Adams Media

New York   London   Toronto   Sydney   New Delhi

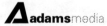

Adams Media
An Imprint of Simon & Schuster, Inc.
57 Littlefield Street
Avon, Massachusetts 02322

ADAMS MEDIA and colophon are trademarks of Simon & Schuster, Inc.

For information about special discounts for bulk purchases, please contact Simon &
Schuster Special Sales at 1-866-506-1949 or business@simonandschuster.com.

Manufactured in the United States of America

10 9 8 7 6 5 4 3 2 1

Library of Congress Cataloging-in-Publication Data has been applied for.

ISBN 978-1-4405-5790-3
ISBN 978-1-4405-3911-4 (ebook)

This work has been previously published in print format by:
Dell Publishing, Inc., New York, NY.

Chapter I

I REMEMBER he hit me with a high right hand about half-way through the seventh round. That's really all Charley ever had, that right hand; it's what kept him from the title and now it was keeping him in beat-out blondes. A great spoiler, Charley had been.

Had been, had been, had been.

I was sure getting the has-beens. Not hundred-percent Punchinellos; they all had some savvy left or there'd be no ink in knocking them over. But there hadn't been a real contender in the string. Max saw to that. Oh, he's sharp—

I'm getting away from the story. I say I remember the high right hand in the seventh, above and in front of my ear.

Then the sun was coming through the full-length windows in this plush Beverly Hills rattrap, and Max was eating corn on the cob. The first week in February, but Max loves corn, even if it's frozen.

He was licking the butter from his fingers and reading the *Times* sport pages and smiling. Max smiles a lot.

"What's so funny?" I asked.

"Me," he said. "Sitting in this snob asylum, eating corn on the cob in February. Me, sitting here with the middle-weight champion of the world, me, Max Freeman. How you feeling, Champ?"

"All right."

It was warm in the room and the warmth was coming from outside, through one of the sliding glass doors. February, and they'd just had the wettest week in a hundred years, but now it was hot.

The suite had its own little enclosed patio where I figured to get a lot of sun, that afternoon. I wanted to rest, to soak up the sun, but mostly to rest.

Max was pouring coffee from a big silver urn. "Ain't we fancy? Max Freeman pouring coffee in his Beverly Hills suite. Ain't this the cat's nuts?"

I heard some people talking in the hall outside, two women. I thought about Sally and asked Max, "What time is it in Chicago now?"

He smiled. "Noon. She's probably just getting up."

Maybe she's taking a shower, I thought, and saw her slim, firm body under the spray, saw her stretching under it, arching toward it, and was jealous of the water that caressed her.

"That seventh round," Max said. "I thought the bum got to you, for a second, there."

"He did," I said.

"Sure, sure. But you damn well went to work on him after that."

"Did I?"

Max had the cup of coffee halfway to his lips. He set it down very deliberately.

His voice was quiet. "Luke—what's wrong? Something's wrong?"

"Maybe I'm punchy," I answered. "It happens to all of us, sooner or later, doesn't it?"

"No," he said. "God damn it, no. I can name you dozens that never— Luke, for God's sake, this is a gag?"

"I don't remember anything after the seventh," I said, "after that high right hand, that haymaker."

His voice was still quiet, which isn't like Max. "After

that—until when, Luke? When can you remember again?"

"Now," I said. "You sitting there, eating corn."

His eyes moved over my face, digging at me. His voice too calm. "I read an article by Tunney once. He had a little exhibition with Eddie Egan. Eddie got to him with a solid one. Gene remembered nothing until next morning, at breakfast. Luke, Tunney's punchy? Like Einstein, he's punchy."

"Keep selling me, Max," I said. "I want to buy."

"You'll rest," he said. "You'll—retire. That's it, step down while you're still champ. That's the classy way to do it." Moisture in his eyes? "But don't worry about a little memory lapse. Just don't worry about a damn-fool thing like that, Luke. It happens to everybody, one time or another."

"I'll bet," I said.

"It's happened to me," he went on. "Often. Must have left fifty watches in washrooms, in my time. Take 'em off to wash my hands, you know—Luke, damn it, quit staring."

"Okay. *Okay!*" I stood up and went out to the patio. I stretched out on the canvas pad of the redwood chaise longue and closed my eyes. I could feel the sun on my eyelids and see the redness of their blood through them.

I'd seen a lot of blood in fifteen years, too much.

Rough linen was being draped over my eyes, a napkin. Max's voice was tired. "You had a couple drinks, you know. It could have been that. It was probably that. You're not much of a drinking man, Champ."

I didn't answer him. I could smell his cigar and hear his feet scrape on the concrete patio, and feel the sun soaking into my body.

A plane droned overhead and tires hummed along the asphalt of Sunset Boulevard and I thought of Sally in Chicago, where it was probably cold, this February day.

The wind comes off the lake, in Chicago, and sweeps along the Outer Drive, along Michigan Boulevard, and throws the sharp snow into your stinging face. The Windy City.

I'd fought Muggsy Ellis there and Joe Lane and Tommy Burke. I'd met Sally there, three winters ago.

Good fight town, Chicago, good girl town.

A party in one of those towering apartments on the near north side, a guy Max knew from the Bronx originally, an artist, sort of. Great big apartment with the bedrooms off the balcony, one of those.

Paintings on the walls I didn't understand, angles and planes and splashes of gaudy color. People I didn't know in knots all around the big room, most of them drinking. A girl sat on the piano bench, looking at her hands, which were in her lap.

Her dress was black wool jersey, her hair was almost white, her eyebrows were as black as the dress.

Max stopped to talk to a couple sports scribes and I kept walking, over to the piano bench.

She looked up and smiled.

"I'm a stranger here, myself," I said. "My name is Luke Pilgrim."

"Hello, Luke," she said. "Where's your tambourine?"

I didn't say anything.

"The name," she explained. "You're an evangelist or something, aren't you, with a name like that?"

"I'm a fighter," I said. "I'm middleweight champion of the world."

Her face quiet, her eyes mocking. "What am I supposed to do, genuflect?"

"I thought maybe you'd talk to me," I said.

A pause, and she patted the bench beside her. "Sit down, Luke, and tell me the thrilling story of your career."

I sat down, and asked, "Are you an actress?"

"No. Aren't we going to talk about you?"

"Not unless you want to. What's your name?"

"Sally. I'm an artist, Luke. Free-lance, commercial. Do you like to fight?"

"Yes. Why?"

"You tell me. Why do you like to fight?"

"I don't know. One of the sports writers claimed I was a sadist, once. Why do you like to paint or sketch or whatever you do?"

"Sublimation of the sexual drive," she said. "I thought all fighters were lumpy-eared and beetle-browed and talked in hoarse whispers."

"A lot of them do and are," I agreed. "I'll probably wind up like that. Is your hair naturally that color?"

"Gray? If I were going to dye it, would I dye it *gray?* Prematurely gray, I add coyly."

"It's very attractive," I said. "You're—striking."

"So I've been told. I've been called everything but beautiful. Why doesn't anyone ever call me beautiful?"

"I don't know," I said, "because you are."

Right from that first minute, she was for me. Her divorce wasn't final at that time, but it didn't stop me from moving in. Her divorce was final now. Why weren't we married?

She claimed she was allergic to marriage. She claimed George had done that to her. He worked for Sears Roebuck. He was blond and tall, and Max shared my opinion of him.

Max said one day, "I wish I could buy him at my price and sell him at his. I'd be richer than Baruch."

And she'd been married to *him.*

Tires hummed and the sun worked into my bones and the smell of Max's cigar stayed with me.

I said, "Where's all the money gone, Max? I haven't enough money to retire."

"Taxes," Max said, "and convertibles and fancy hotels and all your hungry friends. My fault, I suppose. You haven't got any sense; I should have watched your money for you, boy."

"Who'd watch yours?" I asked him. "You're as broke as I am."

"Sure, but I didn't take the punches. Don't worry about money, kid. A pair like us can always make a buck."

"Us?" I said. "You mean you won't be digging up another boy after I retire? You're quitting the game?"

"Why not? I had a champ. How many of them ever get a champ? And especially one like you."

"Aw, Max," I kidded him, "you say the sweetest things."

"I'm your pal," he told me. "You want to tell me about the redhead now?"

I took the napkin off my eyes and stared at him. He was smiling.

"That loss of memory, Luke. A gag, huh? Account of the redhead?"

"You're not making sense," I said.

He took a deep breath. "You left the party with her. Brenda Vane, remember?"

"I don't even remember the party. I don't remember anything after the seventh round. I told you that, Max."

"I know you did, I know you did. I figured it maybe was because—of Sally, and you didn't want to talk about the redhead. Oh, hell, I was just—"

"*Hoping*, Max? Hoping I wasn't punchy?"

"You're *not* punchy. You never trained enough to get punchy. That's where the guys lose their marbles, training."

I swung my feet around and sat up, facing him. "Tell me all about it, from the seventh round on, everything you know."

"You knocked him out in the ninth," Max said quietly.

"I thought you'd killed him, for a second, there. You hit him twice, when he was going down."

I took a breath and looked at my hands.

"You've done *that* before," he said.

"I know. What happened after that?"

"You wouldn't talk to the scribes in the dressing-room. We took a cab from there to the party. It was at Sam Wald's house. That's where you latched onto the redhead."

"And I left the party with her?"

"*We* left the party with her. In her car. She dropped *me* off here. The rest I wouldn't know about."

"Brenda Vane," I said, and shook my head. "Sounds theatrical."

"She was. Her name was probably Bertha Schtunk, originally, but you'd never know it to look at her now."

"I wonder if Sally's home," I said. "She probably is, huh?"

"Probably. It's only twenty-two hundred miles; why don't you phone and find out?"

"She'd like that, wouldn't she? I think I will."

"Tell her you're retiring. Tell her it's time for both of you to settle down."

I stood up. "Think it is? Think I'm through, Max?"

He smiled. "Fighting, yes, for money. Though you can still lick anybody but the good boys. You haven't fought a good boy in three years, Luke."

That hadn't been my idea, fighting the bums. But neither had I kicked about it. I went into the suite to phone Sally.

And she was home. And from two thousand miles her voice could charge me.

"Honey," she said. "You're lonely."

"Yup."

"Me, too. Is it still raining out there?"

"It's over eighty," I told her. "It's setting a new record. It's like Miami."

"Tempt me."

"I love you. I miss you."

"I'll see about a plane. Charley didn't hurt you, did he? Charley never hurts *you*, does he?"

"In the seventh, a little," I told her. "Hurry, kid; see about that plane."

A silence, and then: "Luke, what's wrong?"

"Nothing. Max thinks we ought to settle down. I should retire and we should raise kids. You like the sound of that?"

"I'll see about a plane," she said, and hung up.

I stood there, waiting for it to die down, so Max wouldn't laugh at me, waiting for the excitement to go down before I went back to the patio.

A lot of times she's told me what we have is all physical, that we can't seem to find a communication beyond the physical. I didn't know if it was all physical or not, but I knew it was *all*, whatever it was.

The sun seemed brighter when I came back to the patio and the foliage greener and there was a clean smell to the warm air.

Max had the paper again. "It says here you were a new man in the eighth and ninth rounds. It says you looked like the old Luke Pilgrim, the old killer."

"What do you know about that? They've got to write something, I suppose. That's what they get paid for."

"You're sour. She's not coming out, and you're sour."

"She's coming. I'm not sour. But writers give me a pain in the ass, and especially Los Angeles sports writers."

Max looked at me for seconds, not smiling for a change. Finally, "Luke, what the hell's the matter with you?"

"Maybe I'm sensitive," I said. "Maybe I didn't like your crack about me fighting bums. It wasn't my idea, you know."

"Relax," he said. "Stretch out and get that sun again. Since when are we polite to each other?"

I stretched out on the pad again. "Why did you make that crack about me hitting him twice when he was going? I'm the only boy who ever hit a man on the way down?"

"No. I shouldn't have said it to you, not this morning. It's the way you used to fight, in the old days. Every fight was personal with you then. The last couple of years, you fought a different fight, since—" He stopped.

"Since I met Sally?"

"All right, yes. I'm not kicking. She's done you a lot of good. You're a better man today."

"And a worse pug."

"I like you better this way."

"But the fans don't, and the writers."

"We won't worry about them, not any more," Max said. "We're retiring."

When I was a choir boy at All Saints, when I was ten years old, I boxed with the big gloves. And licked a kid of twelve. In the Golden Gloves, I'd won the novice title the first year and the open title my second.

I'd had seven kayos in a row my first year under Max; in all the years under Max, I had lost one fight, to Jeff Koski in Buffalo. And put him away in the fifth, the next time we met. Jeff hadn't fought again.

Yes, it had been personal in the early days. And why? My family weren't rich, but there had always been food and warm clothes and the Saturday movie. There'd been a full four years of high school. The hungry ones were the killers, usually, the boys from the tough districts.

There wasn't any reason for animosity in me; I just liked to hit them. And I didn't mind taking a punch.

"We'll settle down out here," Max said, "and go into the real estate business, like Dempsey. This is the country for us. Feel that sun?"

For seven years, Max had talked California, but the lure of the Bronx was deep in him.

I said, "We'll keep fighting, Max."

"No, no. No, we're not that hungry."

"The good boys, if there are any," I went on. "I don't want to do it the 'classy' way, Max. I've handed out some lickings; I've got some due me."

"Under another noodle, you'll continue fighting," Max said. "Not under me."

"Art Cary," I suggested. "We could pack the Polo Grounds with him, Max. We'd make a mint."

Nothing from Max

"Or maybe Patsy Giani," I said.

"Never," Max said vehemently. "Patsy Giani, *never*. Not while I've got anything to do with it, not while I've got a string I could pull."

Patsy was one of the new breed, racketeer-owned. Patsy was a real tough guy and he admitted it. Twenty-six years old and built like a brick outhouse, a natural mauler and brawler. He could have lived and died fighting smokers if the smart, dirty money hadn't taken him over.

"He'd kill you," Max said. "And if he couldn't, they would, sometime after the fight. We want no part of Patsy Giani and his dago friends."

"Italian," I corrected him. "Sally says we shouldn't use words like dago."

"I'm not going with Sally," he answered. "Are you reading your Hemingway, Mr. Pilgrim? You promised Sally you would, this trip."

"Now would be a time for that," I said. "Get it for me, huh, Max? It's in the small grip."

He stared at me.

"Please," I said. "I'm still a little weak from last night."

He smiled. "Oh? You're beginning to remember?"

"From the fight, *the fight*," I explained. "All right, I'll get the book myself." I made a motion toward rising.

"Never mind," he said. "Relax." He got up and went through the door.

When he came back, he tossed me the book. "I'm going out to see if anybody's wearing their sun suits. That sun starts to burn, get out of it."

I nodded, and winked at him.

For Whom the Bell Tolls, a new one to me. I was a little behind in my reading, and Sally would quiz me on it. I read the quotation in the front and wondered if I sent to ask for Patsy Giani, would the bell toll for me?

Traffic hummed and the sun worked and I read. Traffic hummed and the sun went away for a while and I read on.

A chime sounded and I came out of the Hemingway world to this one.

It was a telegram from Sally. She'd be here around seven.

I was on the way back to the patio when the door opened and Max came in. His face was pale; he stared at me with horror and some wonder in his brown eyes. He had a newspaper in his hand.

"What's wrong, Max? You sick?"

"I'm sick. We're in trouble, kid." He waved the paper at me. "Nobody's been here—no—cops?"

"Hell, no. What is it, what's the story?"

He looked past me. "The clerk, damn it—" He turned toward the door. "I'll be back." He threw me the paper. "Read that, and ask if we're in trouble." The door slammed behind him.

There was a picture of a girl on the front page, a girl with a badly battered face. She was wearing a negligee from which one breast was about to emerge. She was sprawled awkwardly on what seemed to be a studio couch, her puffed mouth hanging open, her dead eyes staring.

The headline read: *Model Found Slain.* The story under the headline identified her as former B girl who had recently enjoyed exceptional success as a photographer's model and had been offered a contract by a small producer.

It was a Hearst paper and the writer called this *the promise of a new and fabulous career cut short by the brutal hand of a lustful and vicious killer.*

The girl's name was Mary Kostanic.

But her professional name was Brenda Vane.

Chapter II

THIS WAS THE GIRL I'd left the party with. I stared at the battered face, but there was no memory stir, no recognition in my mind at all.

Behind me the door opened, and I turned to see Max standing there.

"He's not on now," Max said. "He won't be on until six tonight."

"Who?"

"The desk clerk. The man I got our key from last night."

"Why do you want him?"

"I want to tell him you and I came home together. I want to find out if he remembers that."

"No, Max," I said. "We aren't buying anybody. We're going into this clean. This is murder, Max."

"You're telling me this is murder. How stupid can you get, Luke? You going to tell the cops you were with her, but you don't know where, or how long? You going to tell 'em you can't remember how you left her? That's some story, isn't it? They'll buy that."

"It's the truth."

"Is it? How do you know you were with her? Maybe I lied to you. Maybe I killed her and I was trying to cover, this morning. Did you think of that?"

"Simmer down, Max," I said wearily. "You're no killer."

"And neither are you. And there'll be two guys swearing you came home with me; me and the desk clerk. I'll do the thinking. Just leave it up to me, kid."

I thought about the sports writers' comments. Last night I'd looked like the old Luke Pilgrim, the killer. Last night, *after* that seventh-round haymaker of Charley's.

"What beats me," Max said, "is why the law hasn't been here already."

I didn't answer.

"Of course," Max went on, "they probably don't know about the party. This paper just came out, and the law'll be getting calls now, I'll bet. They—" He stopped, looking at me thoughtfully.

Then he went to the phone, picked it up. He said, "Will you give me the nearest Los Angeles police station, please?" A pause. "No, not Beverly Hills. This concerns the Los Angeles police. Hurry, please."

I went over to sit near the window. I could see the winding drive that led off Sunset, the cars jamming the parking-lot. Not a clunker in the bunch.

Max was saying, "—just this second saw the afternoon paper, and wanted to tell you I was with the girl around midnight, and . . . Yes, Max Freeman, and I'm at—"

A Jaguar came out from under the portico and headed down toward Sunset. Well-named, that car, like a sleek cat. The man driving it had a goatee and wore a beret.

Max replaced the phone in its cradle and rubbed his hands on his trousers. He expelled his breath noisily. "Beat 'em to the punch, I say. Every angle-shooter at the party will put the bee to us, if we don't. And this town is all angle-shooters."

"I thought you liked this town. You were going to settle here, this morning."

"The town I like, but not the people. Besides—"

"Max," I interrupted, "do *you* think I killed her?"

"Don't talk like a damned fool."

"I could have. I wonder if I'll ever know."

"Shut up. You're getting all wound up, thinking that crap. The law finds out you lost your memory, it won't matter if you did or not. Take it easy now and let me handle this."

I could feel a drop of sweat running down my side.

"You're the middleweight champ of the world, don't forget that. This is a town which goes easy on the names. You're a name. Unless they got a real, solid case, they won't make any rough moves. But don't do any talking."

My right arm jerked. I said, "I'm not as dumb as you think, Max. And you're not as bright. This isn't a fight you're finagling—this is murder."

"That I know. And I'll handle it."

Only one man came, a detective sergeant named Sands. He didn't look like a municipal cop; he wasn't heavy enough, for one thing, and his voice was low-pitched. He would have weighed in as a middle, a tanned, fairly slim man with gray-black hair and dark-blue eyes.

He listened to Max's story without interruption, and then looked at me. "Anything to add?"

I shook my head.

He continued to look at me. "Know the girl long?"

"Met her last night, Sergeant."

Max said quickly, "We both met her last night."

"And she brought you *both* home?"

Quiet in the room, for a second, before Max answered, "That's right, Sergeant."

I was trembling. I looked at the sergeant, and found his eyes on me. Nothing, no words, nothing.

"Why?" Max asked. "Why'd you ask that?"

"Because it isn't what the room clerk said."

"He's a liar, then. He's—"

The sergeant raised a hand. "Take it easy. He's a fight

fan. It isn't likely he'd overlook the middleweight champ. I'm a fight fan, myself." He came over to stand in front of me. "Could I see your hands? The knuckles, please."

The hands trembled, but I held them out for his inspection. Not a mark on them.

I dropped them again, and he said, "You were sure a tiger, those last couple of rounds."

I nodded.

"Do any drinking at the party?"

"A couple, two or three."

"Do much drinking, generally?"

"Very little."

He looked at Max. "I'm going to ask him some questions, now, and I don't want a word out of you, not a single word." He turned back to me. "You face the other way so you can't see him."

I turned in the chair and waited. I wondered if he could hear my heart beat.

He said quietly, "Who was carrying the key?"

"Neither of us. Max got it at the desk."

"And who got into the elevator first?"

I was going to say I didn't remember, but then I thought of his earlier words. He'd mentioned the room clerk, but not the elevator operator. Maybe he was a fight fan, too.

I said, "Neither. We walked up."

I could hear Max's quick intake of breath, and the sergeant must have, too. He glanced quickly at Max, and back to me.

His voice was softly casual. "I want to play along with you, Champ. But I'm all cop, first. A lie, now, would put you in a real rough spot from here on."

"I can't afford to lie," I said, "now or ever."

"And maybe you can't afford not to." He looked over at Max. "Both of you come to the west-side station at four, and fill out your statements. Ask for me; I'll be there."

He paused. "We're keeping this quiet as we can, as long as we can. Boxing couldn't take it, today. But we can't work any miracles."

He didn't say good-by.

Silence in the room, and then we heard the elevator door slam, and Max went to our door and opened it to look down the hall.

When he closed it again, I said, "You should have briefed me. You did walk up last night, didn't you?"

He nodded. "I can't think of everything. I haven't had much experience with murder. They're going to go easy, you know that? It's the title, and we've always been cleaner than most, and they're going to go easy."

"The man's all cop," I answered. "He said that, and I believe him. He's all cop, and smart."

"We're dumb?"

"We're dumb in lots of ways. I wish Sally was here. She's not dumb any way."

Max looked at me bleakly. "She's got a lot of reading behind her. A hell of a lot of good that'll do us in this mess."

"She'll think of something," I said. "I don't want to think about it any more, Max."

"No, you never want to think. I spoiled you. Aach—" He went over to slump on a love seat.

I left him there, staring at the carpet, while I went in to take a hot, hot shower. I was itchy and jumpy and the cool eyes of Sergeant Sands were still in my memory.

If he was going easy on us, it was because of orders from upstairs. I had the feeling that Sergeant Sands wasn't even easy on himself.

The needle shower dug at me and steam filled the shower stall. My mind went reaching back for last night, trying to find a frame for the picture of Mary Kostanic, alias Brenda Vane. Somebody had really worked on that face. Me?

Killer Pilgrim.

I was shaving when the phone shrilled. The bathroom door was open now, and I could see Max at the phone. I could hear, "Yeah. Right. Sure I know him. Jesu-us!" Max turned to look my way and shook his head. "Course. We'll be there as quick as we can make it."

I had stopped shaving, and I came out now into the sitting-room.

"Charley Retzer," Max said. "In a hospital. Been unconscious since they picked him up on the street at eleven last night."

"*I* did that to him?" I said. "Or a car? What is it?"

"Not you," Max said quickly. "You and everybody else who's ever hit Charley. But it was your name he remembered when he came to. We've got time, but it'll be a rat race. From there to the station and then to eat and then the airport. Why'd they phone *us?*"

"Easy, Max. Slow down."

He took a deep breath.

I said evenly and slowly, "We can miss Sally at the airport and we can miss the session at the station. But we've got to see Charley. That's the one important thing."

"All right. *All right!*"

I went into the bedroom to dress, and Max followed me in. He said wearily, "Since when are you getting sentimental? Think of the times he's gouged you and butted you and elbowed you and open-handed you. If you're going to get soft, why Charley?"

"The way he fought was the way he learned to fight," I said. "There wasn't anything personal in it; it was just a way to win. Max, he's one of ours. He's our kind of bastard."

"Yeah, I guess. God, that battle he had with Zale, huh?"

All guts and blood, that one. I said nothing.

"And Graziano, too. He never ducked anybody, did he?"

"Not even Patsy Giani," I said meaningly.

"No, but I'll bet he wishes he had. I thought Giani killed him that night."

"He didn't even put him in the hospital," I said.

Max said nothing to that. He shook his head and went back to the other room.

Charley in the hospital and Brenda Vane dead and Mr. Pilgrim reading Hemingway in the bright sunlight. Me and Tunney, readers. Maybe I could work up to Shakespeare, like Gentleman Gene.

I'd rather be Harry Greb, Jr.

We rented a car, a Cadillac. Max thinks he's another Walt Faulkner, and a Caddy convertible is his idea of a hot heap. In this town they're like Chevs in Detroit.

The sun was still up there as he wheeled it through the Sunset afternoon traffic. His face was gray and his hands were tense on the wheel. He had some unrepeatable words for the driving-habits of every unfortunate who happened to get in front of us.

Great little man for a crisis, Max Freeman, steady as a house of cards. It was a good thing Sally was on the way.

The hospital was in West Los Angeles, right off Westwood Boulevard. It was a rest home, really, a small place that couldn't have held more than ten patients, top. It looked like one of those alcoholics' purse-traps to me.

And probably to Max. His nose was wrinkling as we went up the three concrete steps to the front porch. A small brass plate on the door invited us to enter, which we did.

A carpeted hallway, with glass doors leading off to the left, with an open stairway making the wall to our right. The glass doors led to a fairly large carpeted room that held two desks and a variety of living-room furniture.

A gray-haired man in a white jacket was sitting at one of the desks, going over some charts. He had the build of

John L. Lewis, but not the eyebrows. The eyebrows were thin white lines over a pair of bloodshot blue eyes.

He rose as we entered. He asked, "Mr. Pilgrim?"

"I'm Luke Pilgrim, Doctor," I said. "This is my manager, Max Freeman."

He shook our hands. He said, "I'm Doctor Drinkwater. Mr. Retzer is going to be all right."

There was relief in Max's voice. "What was it? What knocked him out?"

Dr. Drinkwater permitted himself a small smile. "Mr. Pilgrim, I believe, in the ninth round. And after that, some whisky."

Max's smile was as frosty as the doctor's. "Could we see him, now?"

"Of course. Room eight, right at the top of the stairs, there."

Going up, Max said, "Mr. Pilgrim, I believe, in the ninth round. I'll bet he thought he was Milton Berle, getting that one off. Drinkwater, what a name for a dipso quack!"

"You just don't like to be the straight man, Max. I didn't know Charley drank."

"There ain't anything Charley hasn't done," Max said. He paused at the top of the stairs, and looked at the door to room eight, which was partially open. He seemed nervous.

I went ahead of him and pushed the door open, and Max followed me in.

Only Charley's head was visible; the rest of him was covered by a heavy dark-blue wool blanket.

He looked our way and grinned. One eye was puffed shut, and the whole left side of his face seemed to be out of place, but the grin was genuine.

"Hey, Champ, hello! And Maxie."

"You were asking for me, Charley," I said. "I didn't

know you cared."

"Asking, hell, I was *looking* for you, Champ. Man, you never did *this* to me before." And then suddenly serious: "What the hell came over you, Luke, in those last two rounds?"

I was now standing next to him. "I don't know, Charley. That high right hand you landed in the seventh, and I guess I went nuts."

"You sure did." He looked past me at the wall. "First time in thirteen years I was kayoed, Luke. The only time since I've been a pro."

"Good time to quit, Charley," I said quietly. "I'll be quitting myself, I think. Maybe one more. With Giani."

"Don't be simple, Luke. Patsy'd kill you. He's a bull. He's a tiger."

"Maybe. Let's talk about you. What happened to you?"

"Shame, I guess. Damn it, Luke, you butchered me. For these West Coast yokels. I figured some easy bucks, old Luke Pilgrim, just a show for these hicks. And then you made like Graziano. I've been your screen, Luke. I've kept a lot of good boys from ever getting to you. I saved you from a lot of young men's punches. I—"

"And you've thumbed me and gouged me and butted me and worse," I interrupted. "Quit talking like Grantland Rice."

His grin came back. "All right. Hey, Luke, remember Jersey City, in the fifth?"

"That was the closest you ever came," I agreed. "And you stalled. You could have walked in and put me in the three-dollar seats. You sure had a baboon in your corner that night."

"Doc Heinrich," he remembered. "Old Safe and Sane. He cost me the title, that pinochle hound."

Max said, "Doc was all right. Doc's dead, remember."

"He should have died earlier," Charley said, *"before*

Jersey City. What a knot-head."

"Please," Max said. "The man's dead. Please—boys."

"So's Hitler," Charley said. "You mourning him, too, Max?"

Max was silent, wearing his patient, sad expression.

Charley's good eye winked at me. "You got the cream of the noodles, Champ. If I'da had Max, I'd be wearing the crown right now."

Max said nothing, but he couldn't keep the smugness from his face.

I said, "Maybe you'd better rest, Charley. Going to be here long?"

"Get out tonight, or tomorrow morning. It was just the whisky, I guess. Though this quack hasn't told me for sure."

"We'll be seeing you, then," I said. "Call us when you're ready to go."

"Sure. We'll go quail-hunting. This is the town for it." His voice changed. "Luke, don't take on Patsy. He's murder, Luke, pure murder."

"We'll see," I said. "Don't fret about it. Get well, kid."

"Yeh," Max said. "Rest. Don't worry about Luke. He fights Giani, it won't be under me."

We went right from there to the west-side station, to a small room with Venetian blinds, the blinds closed against the glare of the day outside.

Sergeant Sands was there with two other men. One was a uniformed cop with a sheaf of papers, the other was a big, redheaded gent in a cheap and wrinkled suit.

Sands said, "Sergeant Krivic will take your statements." Those words and the glance was all he was allowing us at the moment.

Sergeant Krivic was the uniformed man. He took our statements and had them typed up, and we signed them.

Sands was at a desk in one corner of the room, watching

us as we signed. He waved us over without getting up.

We came there and stood in front of the desk. We were like a couple of kids before their high-school principal.

"You'll be in town for a while?" he asked, after a second.

"I guess," Max said. "Hard to tell."

"Call me if you intend to leave. Check with me first."

"All right, Sergeant," Max said.

Sands looked at me. "Anything to say, Mr. Pilgrim?"

"Nothing. That's what Max gets paid for, talking."

"And keeping you out of trouble?"

"That's right, Sergeant."

"Okay. I'll be in touch with you. Good afternoon."

"Clean," Max whispered to me, as we went out. "We're clean, clean, clean."

When Max wants to believe something, he keeps repeating it to himself.

"They haven't even given it to the papers," he went on. "They know we're clean and they don't want to dirty the title. Boy, I'm glad that's over."

We were going through the hall now, and at the door a man looked up and said, "Hello, Max. Parking-ticket?"

"Speeding," Max said. "How's by you, Al?"

"Good. Where'd they nail you, Max?"

"Sunset. Sunset and—Rodeo."

We went out, the man's stare following us.

"Reporter?" I asked Max.

"Yup, and a nosy one."

"I like the way you think on your feet," I said. "We're walking out of a Los Angeles police station, and you tell him you picked up the ticket at Sunset and Rodeo."

"So?" He was climbing into the Cad.

"That's in Beverly Hills." I climbed in and slammed the door. "Maybe I'd better do the thinking from here in. I couldn't do much worse than you've done today."

Nothing from him. And nothing from me. Behind me

was a blank I couldn't fill, but which could be full of horror. Ahead was Sally. And, I felt sure, future attention from Sergeant Sands.

Max knows his way around the fight game, but on other things how wrong he can be.

The traffic was thick, and Max was giving it all his attention.

"I'm hungry," I said. "How about you?"

"I can eat. Know a good spot for a steak." He continued to look straight ahead. "Maybe I should have let you handle the whole thing. Now that you can read, you're probably brighter than when I first picked you up."

"Where's this steak spot?" I asked.

"On Wilshire. I keep thinking of you as a dumb pug who was a sucker for any slob with a hook. I keep remembering how you looked against Jeff Koski, that first time. And how you thought brown shoes would go all right with your first tux. I keep forgetting about this new influence in your life."

I yawned.

He swung the Cad onto Westwood Boulevard, heading for Wilshire. "You're still a sucker for a high right hand, but you can't learn everything, I suppose. *Nobody* would call *you* dumb."

I stretched my shoulders, arching the ache out of my back.

"I took you from the Gloves to the crown, and there's hardly a mark on you. But, of course, you learned that from Hemingway. Or maybe from Somerset Maugham? Or could it be this Truman Capote taught you that?"

"Okay, Max," I said. "You win. Just one question, and I want it straight, Max."

"Shoot," he said, his eyes ahead, his full face stern.

"Where was it, again, that you got that ticket for speeding?"

Nothing, at first, and then he started to smile. And then he laughed, and I was laughing with him. And then I stopped laughing.

The girl dead, and maybe I killed her. What did I have to laugh about? I couldn't see myself as a killer, but that's because I'd never killed. The army was full of boys who'd never killed—before.

· The steak was tops. That's another thing Max knew, where the good food was in practically every town in America. The purse-size Duncan Hines.

And people, too, Max knew. There were a couple in here, and we got to gassing in the bar, and the hands of the clock went around without our noticing.

We had to log. Max took Sepulveda and had me pressing the floor boards all the way. When we parked on the big lot, Max looked at his watch triumphantly.

"Three minutes to spare," he said. "I'm some wheeler, eh?"

"You sure are."

Overhead, the big boys were coming in from the east and the west, from the north. Sally was on one of those, and I'd have to tell her about the redhead.

Since I'd met Sally, she'd been enough for me; there'd been no out-of-town sessions since I met her. But there'd been one last night.

The girl was dead; I wondered if that fact would be as important to Sally as the fact that I was with her, dead or alive. I don't scare easily, for some reason, but I was scared now.

Max said, "Well, let's go. That plane's due, Luke."

I got out slowly, and we walked over toward the biggest of the buildings in this immense airport.

Sally's plane wouldn't be in for twelve minutes, the girl at the desk downstairs told us. We went up to the flight deck.

The bar and restaurant was up here, but we stood out on the open part, watching them come in. There were others up there and probably only a few of them were meeting people.

"Like the peasants in the hick towns," Max said, "hanging around the station for the trains to come in and go."

Only this was different. This was an international airport and those big birds were coming from South America and the Orient and Australia, besides all the traffic from the east.

"Some day," Max said, "it'll be Mars and the moon, rocket ships. I wish I wasn't so old."

Well, it was like this, Sally, if I'd known what I was doing, you know I'd never—

Max said, "You cold? What you all hunched up like that for? It's not that cold."

"I'm cold," I said. "Thinking about Sally."

"What d'ya mean?"

I said, "She isn't going to like hearing about the redhead."

"Who's going to tell her?"

"I am."

"Are you crazy? Why? Why should you tell Sally about the redhead? And what can you tell? Look, Luke, the less people know about what I told you, the better. Think of me, if you don't want to think of yourself. Don't be a damned chump."

I didn't argue with him. I was going to tell her, no matter what he said. Her flight was announced, and we went downstairs to wait.

She was wearing a tan suède coat, and no hat. She was carrying a big suède purse and looking worried and expectant. Then she saw me and she started to run.

My arms were waiting for her. My arms went around her and that fine body was pressing mine and I could smell her perfume and feel the softness of her cheek nuzzling my neck.

"I'm starved," she said. "Oh, baby, I've been lonely."

"We can eat upstairs," I said. "If it's food you're starved for. How was the trip?"

"The trip was standard. Food's one thing I'm starved for. Hello, Max." She patted his cheek, the other arm still around my neck.

"It must be love," Max said. "Hello, Sally. How's Chi?"

"Cold, cold, cold." She took my hand and put it into one of the big pockets of the suède coat, holding it there. "Lord, you've got my combination, you—you—"

"Handsome bastard?" I suggested.

"Oh, no," she said. "That's one thing nobody would call you." Her voice suddenly quieter. "Luke, is something wrong?"

"Mmmm-hmmm. We'll talk about it while you eat. Max and I will have a cup of coffee and tell you about it."

"Not me," Max said. "I don't want to be there when she goes through the roof. I'll go into the bar."

"Roof?" Sally stopped walking and looked at me. "Is there a—woman involved in this trouble?"

"I guess so," I said. "I don't remember her."

"You were drunk?"

I shook my head. "Slug-nutty. Let's get something to eat."

We walked quietly into the dimly lighted restaurant. Conversation in the background and the hum of the big birds and the clink of a dish here and there. But from Sally, only the chill silence.

My hands were clammy; my stomach was a knot. Without Sally, nothing would be fun. Without her, I'd just as soon be dead. I would be.

She ordered a steak, and I told her what Max had told me. Max had gone into the bar. I told her about Sergeant

Sands and our story, watching her face for a reaction every second I was talking.

In the dim light her gray hair was silver, her fine eyebrows black as soot. In the dim light there wasn't a trace of expression on her face.

Her steak came, and she just looked at it. She continued to look at it while she said, "Conscience, maybe. A psychic block—because of what happened. Maybe you didn't kill her, but you— What'd she look like? Oh, damn you—"

"I don't know. There's a picture of her in the paper, but she's—it's—I mean, the face was battered."

"Damn you," she whispered. "Damn you, damn you—"

"Sally," I said, "for God's sake, I'm as sick as you are. Infidelity's bad enough, but maybe I *killed* her, Sally."

"Some damned tramp," she said, "some—"

I raised my voice. "Sally, the girl's *dead.*"

She was breathing hard, and her eyes burned at me. "So am I. So are you, in my book."

"Slow down," I said quietly. "Try to be civilized. Get on top of your ridiculous temper. We're not kids, Sally."

She took a deep breath.

"Eat," I told her. "And think. There's never been anybody in my life since the first time I saw you. I don't even want to *look* at other girls. You know that's true."

She ate. Like the mechanical woman; the knife, the fork, the clamp of the jaws, the sip of water. The eyes not meeting mine, the lovely face blank.

Coffee, and she said, "Max. Max and his damned parties. He knows them all, doesn't he, all the tramps?"

"He knew an artist in Chicago, thank God," I said.

"You're getting better with words, aren't you? You know just what to say, don't you?"

"I read a lot," I said. "My girl's got me reading."

"Not last night," she said. "No book, last night; you curled up with a good blonde."

"I don't know," I said. "I don't know what I did last night. The girl who died was a redhead."

She groped through her purse and came up with a cigarette. She lighted it, and stared at her coffee cup. There was some moisture in her eyes. The hand holding the cigarette trembled.

I said, "I like to think nothing happened. Maybe nothing *did* happen while I was with her."

"You like to think."

"Yes. It doesn't make sense, I suppose."

"It doesn't. Luke, I don't want to talk about it now. Maybe tomorrow we'll talk about it. Or maybe I'll get the first plane back tomorrow. But for now, I want to get a room and be alone."

"All right. You may as well stay where we're staying."

I paid the bill and got Max from the bar. Then we went down and picked up her luggage. No dialogue through this; it wasn't a time to crawl and I'm not very good at it, anyway.

Max tried a couple of conversational openings and gave it up. It was a wordless ride, all the way to the hotel.

There she signed a registry card, and a bellhop took the luggage from us. There she said coolly, "I'll leave you here, boys. I'll get in touch with you in the morning—if I haven't gone back to Chicago by then."

"All right," I said, and nothing more.

We were still standing at the desk when she disappeared into the elevator.

Then Max turned to look at the desk clerk. "You were the man on duty when we came in last night, weren't you?"

Chapter III

HE WAS A SLIM MAN, about thirty, one of those blasé types the hotel business seems to attract.

He gave us the guest smile and said, "I believe I was, sir."

Max studied him like a trophy in a game room. "Sergeant Sands claims you told him I came in alone, last night."

"I've been asked not to discuss that, sir."

"Asked by who?"

"By Sergeant Sands."

I said, "I'm tired, Max. I'm going up."

"I'll be up later," Max said.

I didn't argue with him. He was probably going to try and buy something from the clerk, which could really put us in the soup. But I'd had my fill of arguing today.

I was tired, but I knew I wouldn't sleep. My tiredness was nervous tension; it was only nine o'clock and I'd slept late this morning.

The paper Max had bought was still in the room; I picked it up and started to read about Mary Kostanic, alias Brenda Vane.

There was a knock at the door, and I said, "Come in."

Sally.

I said nothing. She said nothing. Very reserved, very calm, both of us.

Finally she said, "Have you a paper that tells about— this—this business?"

"Right here." I stood up and brought it over to her. "You can order more. Are you back to normal now?"

She took the paper and went out.

She was weakening. It was going to be all right. I would have given odds, right then, she wouldn't be on any plane in the morning.

I was sitting by the window, watching the traffic on Sunset when Max came in.

"Well?" I asked.

"Well, what?"

"Did he sell? Did you buy him?"

"Didn't try," Max said. "Want to play some gin?"

"No. What about the clerk, Max?"

"Nothing about the clerk. Where's the paper?"

"Sally came and got it. I've got some books, if you want to read."

"I don't want to read books. What you got against gin rummy all of a sudden?"

"Sit down and relax," I told him. "*I'm* the guy who went with her, not you. You're not in trouble."

He sat down. "If you're in trouble, I'm in trouble. Sands was back here tonight, talking to the help."

"That's what you bought."

"Not from the clerk. That Sands is one of those smooth and easy characters that never gives up and never makes a bum move, I'll bet. That's the way he strikes me. They wouldn't put no punk on a kill like this."

"He's only a sergeant," I said.

"Politics. That's got nothing to do with efficiency. He isn't the kind would butter up to the brass. He scares the hell out of me, so polite and tricky."

"Max," I said, "if it's all right with you, I'd rather not talk about it. Maybe tomorrow, but no more today."

"All right, all right." He rubbed one ear with a flat hand, and stared out at nothing. "I think I'll take a hot bath. My nerves are jumping."

I went back to watching the Sunset traffic. Some people like a view from their windows—trees and lawns, mountains, or water. My view had always been traffic, a great sedative.

The phone startled me.

A man's voice said, "Max?"

"He's in the tub," I said. "Can I help? This is Luke."

"Sam Wald, Luke. You boys will be home for a while?"

"All night. Coming over?"

"Mmmm-hmmm. Like to talk to both of you."

"We'll be here."

Sam Wald? Then I remembered that's where the party had been last night. I went into the bathroom to tell Max about it. He was toweling himself.

Max frowned. "Didn't he say what he wanted to talk about?"

I shook my head.

"What could it be but the—what happened last night? What else would he want to talk about?"

"I don't know. What's his business?"

"Angles. Anything that's got a buck in it is his business. What the hell?"

"Better take another bath, Max," I said. "Your nerves are jumping again."

"You're cool enough, aren't you?" he said. "You've got an awful cold streak in you, Luke."

"Somebody has to have the poise in this combination," I said, and went back to the living-room. I didn't seem to be what is known as a popular champion, at the moment.

Sam Wald was a man of about forty, tanned and looking solid, the handball type. He wore some fine tailoring in blue garbardine and one of those insurance-salesman smiles.

He told us, "Krueger wants a fight for his boy. He came to see me this afternoon."

Dutch Krueger was Giani's manager.

"Why'd he come to you?" Max asked.

Wald shrugged. "He knows we're pretty close."

Max studied him before saying, "Why doesn't he go to the Association?"

Wald shrugged again. "He knows he hasn't too much standing with the N.B.A. The thing is, Max, I've got a piece of that new arena we're building in the Valley and a title fight would be a fine opening attraction."

"I don't want any part of Giani," Max said flatly.

"Maybe I do," I said.

"Go read a book," Max said. "I'll handle this."

I winked at Wald. "That's going to be some arena. Could press a lot of hay into that spot, I'll bet. And there's tons of money being spent out here."

Wald nodded. "I just wish I had Santa Anita's breakage. Great sport town." He paused. "Great gambling town."

The pause made the last three words hang in the room.

I said, "How would you bet that one, me and Giani?"

Another one of his theatrical pauses. Then, "I don't know. Patsy's young and rough and strong. But you're— you're a right smart lad. In a ring, anyway."

Max said, "Let's not talk in circles. We don't fight Giani unless we're ordered to. The way I see it right now, Luke's going to retire. Undefeated."

"Okay," Wald said. "Glad to see somebody's solvent enough to sneer at a big wad of dough. Just an idea I had, Max." He stood up. "Get home all right, last night?"

Silence, and then Max's flat voice: "Why not?"

"Wondered. The desk clerk tells me you were carrying quite a load."

"I'll have to report him," Max said evenly, "talking about the guests like that."

"Not *guests*. *Guest*. He only mentioned you, Max. Well, I'm keeping you boys up, I guess. Good night."

"Sleep tight," Max said. "Dream up another angle, Sam. When did you buy into Giani?"

"I haven't yet," Wald answered. "But he's a comer, Max. That would be a gilt-edged investment."

"So long," Max said, and I nodded. Neither of us stood up.

The door closed behind Wald, and Max looked at me. "He was mentioning Giani last night, at the party. I wouldn't be surprised if that's why he threw the party."

"We could pack that arena," I said.

"Sure. Look, even if I thought you could win, I don't want Patsy's friends on top, not in this division. Not while I'm alive."

"If I could win, they wouldn't be on top," I pointed out.

"You're splitting hairs," Max said. "I wonder if— Oh, who in hell can figure these damned angle-shooters?"

"You. Who was at the party, Max?"

"Some pugs, some sports writers, some broads, couple studio slobs. The kind of people Sam would know."

"I thought he was one of your friends."

"I've got millions of friends," Max said. "Some of them are bound to be heels."

"I'll play gin rummy now."

"No. Not now. I've got to think, kid. Wheels are turning. You hear that crack he made about the clerk, and about betting? We're being squeezed, boy."

"So I fight Giani, and beat his brains out, and all our problems are solved."

"Six years ago," Max said, "you'd have killed him. But this isn't six years ago. Go to bed and let me worry this out."

I went to bed. Cool guy I am, cold. But I lay awake a long time, listening to the hum of tires on the asphalt and the beat of my heart. Thinking of Sally and the redhead and Sands and Sam Wald, thinking of the battered face.

Fell asleep and dreamed I was back in the All Saints choir, the boy soprano. Only my voice was changing and they were grooming Patsy Giani to take my place. Patsy looked like an angel in the blue robes and Buster Brown collar, and I screamed at him, "You're no angel, you're an angle," and woke up to the sound of Max's snoring and the chill clamminess of the perspiration-dampened sheet beneath me.

No hum of tires, dark in the room. A horn bleated, and silence. Max's snore turned into a gurgle, and he muttered something in his sleep.

I looked up into the void overhead, trying to picture a life without the crown, without the big money, without Sally. Tried to look into the void that was last night.

Nothing. Psychic block, because of conscience— I was a long way from All Saints. Where's your tambourine? *You know, Luke,* Sally had once said, *these religious fanatics and these ring tigers have a lot in common. Hitler could have been either, given the build or the bent.*

I rolled over, seeking a dryer part of the sheet. If Sally took a plane tomorrow, I'd be on the next one. I'd crawl, crawl, crawl, and beg.

Max was snoring again, and the rhythm of it got to me, and I went back to sleep.

Sunlight and the sound of the shower. A bath last night and a shower this morning; Max was getting soap-happy. He must feel dirty.

I stretched and considered the ceiling and thought of yesterday, which had been bad. Today could be worse if Sally took a plane.

Max came in, wearing a terry-cloth robe, and the smile

was back. "Another beautiful day," he said.

He'd dreamed up some answers; he looked ready again, on top of all his problems.

"I ordered breakfast," he said. "It'll be here in fifteen minutes. Better get up." His smile got cute. "Breakfast for the three of us. Sally phoned she'd be over."

"To say good-by?"

"Who knows? Get off the dime, boy; it's a beautiful day."

Fully dressed and fully composed she was, when she came for breakfast. Black jersey hugging that fine body, civil reserve clothing her warm voice.

She'd read all the papers, she informed us. The girl had *some* history. There was a better picture of her in the *News* than the one I'd seen. Some build, the girl had.

"She's dead," I said.

Sally nodded, looking at me. I felt like I was on a glass slide.

Max said, "You think those drinks could have been doctored at Sam's?"

I shook my head.

Sally looked at him sharply. "Why? What does this —Sam have to do with it?"

Max looked at me, and I said, "Nothing."

She continued to look at me.

I continued to say nothing.

She asked, "Is he saying there's a possibility you were maneuvered in some way—framed?"

"No," I said. "The lights went out during the fight, not after. Wald may have picked up some information and is trying to use it, but I'm sure he didn't finagle anything."

"And nothing's come back? *Nothing?*"

"Nothing."

Some emotion in her voice now. "Luke, you wouldn't lie to me, would you? *Never*, would you?"

"Never. Not to you, Sally."

"And if you should remember, you'd tell me?"

"I would." I watched her, waiting for the breakdown, waiting to move in for the big clinch, but her composure was back.

"I won't be taking the plane this morning," she said.

Annoyance burned in me; this duchess act could be overworked.

"I'll want a car this morning," she went on. "You and I are going to take a ride, Luke."

"Where?"

"Out to the Palisades, to that place on Sunset."

"Place?" I stared at her.

"The girl's apartment, where she was killed."

"Like hell," Max said. "The joint will be crawling with cops. How would that look?"

"It will look like we're interested. Isn't it logical for a person who was with the victim the night she was killed to be interested in where she lived, and died?"

"I don't know if it's logical or not," Max said, "and neither do you. We could ask Luke."

"It's logical," I said. "Any other questions?"

Sally ate her grapefruit, Max his eggs, and I my buckwheat cakes. Max looked sour, Sally grave. Nobody said anything for seconds.

Then Max said, "I wash my hands of the whole thing. Forget I was ever involved."

"I will if Sergeant Sands will."

Sally said, "They were *your* friends, Max, not Luke's."

He nodded, not looking at her.

Her voice was cool. "You'd be thirty-five-percent involved anyway. Isn't that your usual cut?"

Max's look was ice. "You're hot at me. But I didn't introduce that redhead to Luke. Lay off me."

Her face was stiff as she held his stare. Then her eyes

dropped, and she continued to eat silently.

I was uncomfortable. They were my two closest friends, and their quarreling embarrassed me. But I couldn't think of anything helpful to say.

Max left before we were ready to go. He had some shopping to do, he said.

Sally said, "I was mean to him, wasn't I?"

I nodded.

"I'm too much in love," she said. "You can kiss me now."

I kissed her. No life in her, no response.

"I'm sorry," she said. "I should be mourning the girl. I'm only hating her."

"Maybe we didn't even hold hands," I said. "Nobody knows."

"Maybe," she said, "but it's out of character. Phone for a car, will you?"

We got a Ford convertible. Sally drove. Through Beverly Hills, the wind of Sunset past the big homes, her eyes quietly on the traffic.

As the buildings of UCLA appeared to our left, she said, "Anything familiar?"

"Nothing."

"You drove out in her car, didn't you?"

"That's what Max says."

"And then how did you get back to the hotel?"

"I don't know," I said, without thinking. And then realized that was a hell of an important question.

"If," I said slowly, "she drove me back, I didn't kill her. And if I took a cab, the cabbie would remember. And if somebody else took me—"

"A lot of 'ifs,' aren't there? And you or Max never considered any of them. Max is no help to us, Luke, not in something like this. It would have been better, probably, to tell the police exactly what happened."

"I didn't know what happened. I could go to the gas chamber, not knowing. What kind of a defense would I have?"

She took a deep breath, and didn't answer. She was stopped for the light, and there was a Caddie alongside. The man behind the wheel was a big lug. He looked at Sally and smiled.

Her face froze, and he continued to smile.

"Even out here, you're something," I told her. "I'd go over and pop him, but a boxer's fists are considered a lethal weapon in this state."

"What a horrible thing to say," she said, "after—"

I'd never even thought of it. I just couldn't get used to the thought of myself as a murderer. Murderers probably can't, either.

The light changed, and the Ford jumped. The Caddie turned left. Sally said, "If I didn't have reason to know better, I'd think you were the coldest man alive."

"It's a carry-over from the ring," I said. "Control. In every fight, I try to hold the control. I figure if I lose that, I'll lose the fight."

"It's hard for you, though? It's hard for you to stay cool?"

"Yes."

"All your training has been for the ring. Your attitude toward everything is conditioned by the ring."

"I suppose."

"To hit another human being, to hurt him, perhaps permanently."

"I guess that's right. One thing, though. Without malice."

"You like to believe. All of the real fighters had malice enough, all of the hitters. It's personal, with them."

"I try not to make it personal." My hands were trembling. Sally likes to dig at me, sometimes, and it hurts more than it should. "I get the feeling you don't like me when you talk like that."

We were moving through Brentwood now. She asked, "Remember anything?"

"Nothing."

Past the polo field, past the entrance to Will Rogers Park. The sun was hot in a clear sky, and there was quite a lot of traffic going our way, toward the ocean.

To our left now, the Uplifters, and we were going up-hill. I thought something stirred in my memory but it was a flash of nothing.

We topped the hill and a small sign at the side of the road read: *Pacific Palisades*. New homes along Sunset, on the left here, and then the theater and the start of the business district.

At the west end of the three-block business district, there was a new supermarket. On the face of this building, there was a bakery trade-mark, a small, revolving Dutch wind-mill.

"I've seen that before," I said, "that windmill."

Sally slowed the car. "It's all over town."

"Blue, like that," I added. "But—illuminated."

"It's neon tubing; it probably is illuminated at night." She pulled to the side of the road and stopped. "What else does it bring back?"

"Nothing."

"Try, Luke. Keep looking at it."

I said, "It doesn't bring back anything. But it should prove I was out here."

"Or any of a thousand other places with a sign like that." She started the car again, and we were rolling down a grade. A big sign over the Presbyterian Conference Grounds that I'd never seen before, the bright-green hills all around us that I wouldn't see, at night.

About a mile past the end of town, she swung the convertible in a U-turn and pulled up at the curb on the south side of Sunset. There was a four-unit apartment building here of redwood and pastel-yellow stucco, two stories high and looking brand-new.

"The scene of the crime," Sally said, "and there's an apartment to rent, I see. Do you think it could be—"

"No," I said. "Nobody's that bloodthirsty." I stared at the building, trying to fit it into the void. Nothing, nothing.

Sally said, "Let's look at the vacant one."

"Relax," I said.

"Why not? It might work. They're probably all alike. Luke, this isn't as scatterbrained as it may seem."

She opened the door on her side and looked at me. I got out and together we walked up the three steps to the open entryway.

A large woman in white twill shorts was fishing mail out of one of the boxes in the lobby. Her hair was straw-blond and her eyes a vivid blue.

"Could you tell me if the manager is on the premises?" Sally asked her.

The woman shook her head. "He never is, dearie. Was it about the apartment to let?"

Sally nodded. "That's as good an excuse as any."

The woman's smile was knowing. "Oh? Reporters, are you?"

"More or less," Sally said. "I want to do a feature on it, for the Sunday magazine section, and one look at the—scene would help an awful, awful lot."

"I'd like to help," the woman said, "but I got strict orders from Mr. Creash. He's the manager and—"

She stopped talking, looking at the bill in Sally's hand. It was a twenty-dollar bill.

Sally said, "Who'd ever know?"

"Mr. Creash—" the woman said, "and those officers will

probably be back, and—" Her eyes never left the bill.

Sally said, "If they come, you can tell them you *thought* you gave us the key to the vacant apartment. You were on the phone, see, honey, and you couldn't go with us, but you gave us the key. So you'll be clear."

The woman smiled and shook her head. "You writers! I'll get the key. And then phone my daughter-in-law."

It was on the second floor, facing Sunset. The figured drapes were closed, but the room was bright enough, furnished in warm-toned woods and upholstered chairs.

"Provincial," Sally said. "So sweet and cozy, B-girl provincial." Her eyes moved around the living-room scornfully. "Anything click?"

"Nothing."

She walked over to a door and I followed her. It led to a short hall which led to a bedroom. King-sized bed in here with a honey-tone bookcase-headboard and flanking, matching night stands.

The bed wasn't made; the sheets were maroon silk. The bed looked like it had known a recent storm. Sally stared at it for seconds.

Then she said, "If anything should do it, this should."

A tremor in her voice, and one tear on her cheek. My gal Sal; a girl dead and all Sal worries about is whether I'd made her. And I'm supposed to be the cold one.

"It rings no bells with me," I said.

She turned. "Damn you. *Damn* you."

"Maybe you'd better take the plane," I said. "I wasn't exactly the village virgin when I met you, but I've been living the part ever since. You're probably *glad* the girl's dead."

She stared at me. And then said finally, "God, Luke, I *was*. Oh, Luke, what kind of monster am I?"

"I don't know," I said. "Let's get the hell out of here." I turned and started out, but she grabbed my arm.

"Luke, I'm sorry. I've been a twenty-two-karat bitch."

I kissed the top of her gray head and held her shoulders lightly in my hands, saying nothing.

"We'd better get out of here," she said. "It was a stupid idea of mine, anyway."

"I don't think it was stupid," I said, "but we'd better go, all right."

We went back to the living-room, and the eyes of the photograph on the mantel seemed to be watching us. Both of us stood there a second, looking at the soft, appealing face of a younger Mary Kostanic.

"I'll bet she wasn't Brenda Vane then," Sally said. "She was a pretty girl, Luke."

"She was, there," I said. "I wonder how old she was, then?"

"Eighteen, nineteen."

From the doorway behind us, a voice said, "She was a real pretty girl. And look at this place; you can tell she knew good stuff when she saw it. Nothing cheap about Brenda."

We turned to face the big woman in the white twill shorts.

"Was she ever married?" Sally asked.

"Not that I know of. Would you folks like some coffee? I got a full pot on."

I looked at Sally, and she said, "I'd like some."

The woman's apartment was a replica of the one above, but furnished in the four-rooms-for-four-hundred-and-seventy-nine-dollars-name-your-own-terms-including-refrigerator-stove-and-washing-machine Los Angeles too recent American.

But she made it warm with her outsize geniality.

"It better be good coffee," she said, "at twenty dollars." She chuckled. "I feel kind of guilty about that, but not guilty enough to give it back. Were you cheated, dearie?"

"No, I wasn't," Sally said. "You make a fine cup of coffee."

We were in the bright kitchen, sitting at a Formica-top, chrome-legged table. The woman wore a halter with the shorts and it could have served as a hammock for Max.

Sally asked her, "Didn't you hear any racket, any noise that night it—happened? I should think, being right below and all—"

"I was visiting my daughter-in-law, in Culver City," the woman said placidly. "And the Gendrons were out— they're the people in back on this floor—and it could have been there wasn't much noise, anyway. But wasn't it horrible?"

Sally nodded. I nodded. She was a woman who wouldn't need prompting.

"Lived here ever since the building was finished, eight months ago, and never a bit of trouble about the rent or making noise. No dogs, no kids, no parties, a real ideal tenant, Brenda was. I'm sure going to miss her."

"Must have had plenty of—admirers," Sally said.

"Not many for overnight," the woman went on, "though it isn't a thing I worry about. Wouldn't mind a man of my own, if you'll pardon the frankness, and can't see cooking up a storm about them fortunate enough to—" She stopped, and clapped a big hand over her mouth. "I forgot about you being reporters; you won't print that? I'm just too damned mouthy."

Sally smiled. "I'm not exactly a reporter. This Sunday feature writing is almost as much fiction as fact. It's the— the human side of the—the subject I'm supposed to write up, and I never, never speak ill of the dead."

"I'm sure you don't, dearie. I'm not very often wrong about people, and I liked your looks, right off. Is your hair naturally that color?"

"Since I was eighteen," Sally said. "Brenda didn't have

any steady boy friend, then?"

"I just didn't watch that close. I honestly couldn't say. More coffee?"

Sally rose. "Thanks, no. We have to get back to the office. I wonder if the police have any real leads on this?"

"I don't think so. That Sergeant Sands has about talked my arm off, and the questions he asks, it don't seem to me he's got even the tiniest idea of where to start looking. But, of course, you can't always tell with them—"

We were both standing now. We were walking toward the door, and the woman continued to talk. In the open entry, under the stairs that led to the second floor, we stood a moment, while the talk went on. And then she stopped and looked past us.

Three men were coming up the walk. Two of them were carrying things, things that looked like photographic equipment or technical instruments. The third man carried nothing.

The third man was Sergeant Sands.

Chapter IV

THE SERGEANT'S EYES were cool. His glance flicked over me, went to Sally, and came back to me. "Well," he said. "Well, *Champ.*"

One of the men said, "You got the key, Tom? We haven't much time."

Sands nodded at the big woman. "She has one she'll give you. I'll be up later."

They went on, but the sergeant remained immovable. He said, "What is this?" Then, before I could answer, he looked at Sally. "Who are you?"

"Queen of the May," my girl said. "What makes it your business?"

I said quickly, "This is Sergeant Sands, Sally. He's a detective."

"How do you do?" Sally said, and started past him.

"Just a minute," Sands said. "Come on down to the car, both of you."

I thought for a moment Sally was going to refuse, but she followed meekly enough. We sat in the back; he sat in the front, twisted around so he could face us.

He said, "What's the story, this time?" He was looking at me.

"It wasn't my idea," I said. "My girl doesn't want to believe I didn't go home with this Brenda Vane night before last."

He looked at Sally. "Did he? What'd you find out?"

"Nothing." Sally's chin was up, and she was wearing the queenly look.

"And where were you, that night?"

"In Chicago. I just got here, by plane, last night."

"I see." He had a notebook out now. "Your name, please?"

She gave him that, and there were more questions. Her address in Chicago, and her work and people she'd seen there up to the time she left.

Then he nodded at the apartment. "And how long have you been here?"

"A few minutes. I don't know exactly."

He studied us quietly a moment. Then he said, "Sam Wald was over to see you, last night. What did he want?"

"A title fight, for that new arena he's building, in the Valley."

"Oh. Who's the opponent?"

"Patsy Giani."

His eyes appraised me. "You've been ducking Patsy a long time. Wald have a new approach?"

"You'll have to make that clearer, Sergeant," I told him evenly.

"Some club, some lever, some angle. The party was at his house; that's where you met Brenda Vane. The next night he comes over, and you're going to fight Patsy Giani, you're going to commit suicide."

"I didn't say I was going to fight him, Sergeant. Wald wants me to; it's probably why he threw the party." I took a breath. "I'll overlook the crack about suicide."

"You going to fight him?"

"If I can talk my manager into it. If I do, and you've got some money you want to lose, I'd be glad to cover it."

"Okay. We'll forget I hurt your feelings." His grin was sarcastic. "I thought I'd been playing along too much, as it is. Any reasonable cop would have you in the cooler this second. You were with her; the only person who claims you weren't with her when she died is your manager. That's phony enough. Then, two days later, I come out here and find you talking to Mrs. Ketelaar. *Why?*"

Sally said softly, "My fault, Sergeant. *All* my fault. I'm crazy about the ape, and crazy jealous."

"I'll buy that for now," he said, after a second. He looked at me. "Even if you are clean on the murder, it's plain enough to me you're in the middle of it, one way or another. Maybe you don't even know it, and that's why I'm going along, for now." He got out of the car and held our door open. His dark-blue eyes rested on me gravely. "Publicity on this could just about ruin the fight game. It stinks enough, today. I'm still more cop than fight fan, though, and so's the chief. Remember that."

I nodded. Sally nodded. We had no dialogue as we walked to the convertible, as Sally started it, as we moved back Sunset, the way we'd come.

Traffic whizzed by us, the sun glinted off the windshield, the Ford murmured to herself. We went past the turning windmill insignia on the front of the supermarket, and came to a red light against us.

Then Sally looked over at me. "That man gives me the creeps. Relentless, cold, analytical. I thought cops were dumb."

"Only the dumb cops." I turned to look at the Dutch windmill revolving. "Isn't that a silly thing to stick in my memory?"

"It must have some significance, something beyond just seeing it, possibly some—connection with what happened."

The light changed, and we went on.

"And another thing," Sally said, "When I lived out here, I used to know one of the detectives. And he told me

Homicide men *always* worked in a team, two men. *Always,* he said. This case can't be too important, with just one sergeant on it."

"You and Max," I said, "are determined to look at the bright side, the easy side." In my mind I saw the windmill going around and around. "Maybe things have changed, or maybe the other cop is working more quietly. Besides, *I* want to know what happened if—" I didn't finish.

"I don't," she said. "I thought I did, but I don't."

I didn't say anything to that. There'd be only one reason why she wouldn't want to know. The windmill went around and around, trying to tell me something.

Past the Will Rogers Ranch Gate. He'd been something, Will Rogers, and now he was only a memory in middle-aged minds. And some day, Luke Pilgrim, you'll be only ink in a dusty record book. And Brenda Vane, on the threshold of a new career— From B girl to B pictures, the story of Brenda Vane.

Who made it? Even the title, the crown, what the hell was it when you got there? The crown should be something; it sure as hell was when you were a punk, something to look up to. Until you saw what it was made of—a lucky punch here, the right kind of matching, an angle and a wedge and a manager who knew a lot of people.

"What are you thinking of?" Sally asked.

"Oh, nothing much. What's worth while? Where does a man get any real satisfaction?"

"In bed," Sally said. "Both asleep and awake, in bed."

"I'm serious," I said.

"So am I."

Brentwood, and the fine homes. What did they think of, these country-club cuties, besides the bed? And breaking eighty and dashing off to Hawaii for the holidays and money, money, money, money, money?

Sally said, "In your trade, you're at the top. There's

no place to go from where you are. It's not achievement that keeps a man happy, it's achieving."

I'd heard that before.

"When I was younger," she said, "I thought it was love, love, love. With men, I learned, it's love, love, love for however long it takes and then it's a stiff drink and seeing some people. So I said to myself, there's always the memory; relish it while you're making it, and cherish it when it's past, lay it in lavender."

"That's some rat race," I said.

"Luke, there's only *now*."

At All Saints, they'd said there was more than now, but I was eighteen years from All Saints. I was middleweight champion of the world, driving along Sunset with a lovely dish.

"You're going to have to grow up sometime," Sally said.

I should grow up? At sixteen I'd broken another kid's nose. At fourteen I'd learned about women. How long did it take?

"That book you're reading," Sally said, "what scene do you remember?"

"The sleeping-bag."

"Mmmm-hmmm. Mr. Hemingway knows. It's bulls and sex, war and sex, Africa and sex. And sex."

And murder and sex, I thought. But didn't say. I said, "There's a chance he doesn't know everything. Nor anybody else." The windmill went around and around.

"Well, I'll work you up to better, to Thomas Mann and some of the giants. You're going to be well-read, a real civilized gent, fit to share my bed." She was grinning, not looking at me, squinting at the sun and the traffic.

"Silk sheets," she said quietly. "Maroon silk sheets. Doesn't it give you the creeps?"

"No."

A light, and UCLA spread out to our right front. I said, "Turn here. Let's get a drink or a cup of coffee."

"Why here?" she said. "This place has sad memories for me."

"Why?" I looked at her, but she wasn't looking at me.

"This is where George and I spent most of our married life, the first eighteen months of it."

"Turn anyway. I'm hungry."

She turned. Past the campus to our right and left, past the first of the small shops, and here was a parking-space. She parked and looked around.

"It's changed."

"You, too," I said. I got out and put a nickel in the parking-meter. I waited for her on the sidewalk.

She came over to walk along with me. "Wasn't that a ridiculous bed, so big and—Hollywoodish?"

"It's what I'd like."

"Well, you should know. You probably—"

"Shut up," I said. "You're working yourself into a state again."

"All right. Doesn't the thought of George bother you, what he was, and—"

"No," I said.

"It would kill me," she said, "if you'd been married. I'm not very mature, I guess." She reached over and took my hand.

I said, "What I like about you is your steady, unemotional mind. You're so reasonable."

"You shut up." Her hand tightened on mine. "We don't want to fight, not today. It's such a beautiful day."

Quite a change from breakfast.

"George is back in this town," she said. "He has a big job with Sears now. Maybe I should look him up."

"Maybe you should," I agreed. "I don't see any place to

get a drink. Let's eat something."

"I'm not hungry. Isn't this wonderful, for February? I never should have moved to Chicago."

"You should have seen it a week ago, thirteen inches of rain."

"You should have seen Chicago, five inches of snow and seven inches of soot. And twelve below zero. And you out of town." She stopped. "Look at that dress! Isn't it terrific?"

There were two dresses in the window. One was blue silk.

"That blue silk taffeta," Sally went on. "I'm going in. C'mon, I want to see how I look in it."

She was back to normal.

The dress wasn't for her, nor half a dozen others the salesgirl showed her. I got her safely past the next shop and into a restaurant.

We had steak sandwiches and malts. It was near the lunch hour and the place was full of UCLA guys and gals. Chatter, chatter, chatter, yak, yak, yak. Sweater men and sweater girls.

"They'll never again have it so good," I said. "I wish I'd gone to college."

"Why?"

"Oh, I don't know. Background."

"I went. Is my background showing?"

"It shows. You know it shows. You can mix anywhere."

"Light?" she asked, a cigarette in her hand.

I held a light for her, and then she was smiling at me. "You're all right the way you are, Champ. I wouldn't want you any way but the way you are."

"There's been a change in the last couple hours, hasn't there? Even if maybe I am a—"

"Don't," she interrupted quickly. "Don't say it, now."

We went back to the car and she climbed behind the

Wheel again. Past Wilshire, just idly driving and here was another supermarket and another of those revolving Dutch windmills and for a part of a second, something seemed to break through the surface of my mind and then it went away as quickly.

"Damn it," I said.

"Now what?"

"I thought something was going to come back, for a second. But it went away."

"The windmill again?"

"I suppose. Yes."

"Maybe that's where she dropped you, on the way out. Maybe you got fresh and she got indignant. No, that wouldn't be it."

"Stop being nasty," I said. "You were doing fine, up to that crack."

"All right. Luke, I don't want to go back to the hotel, do you?"

"I don't care."

"Luke, do you know what I'm saying?"

I looked at her and knew. "But where?" I asked. "No luggage, the middle of the day. What the hell would a motel think?"

"Motels don't think. And the manager can think what he damn pleases. Luke, it's been a long time."

It had been two weeks. I said, "Turn back to Wilshire. Wilshire's loaded with motels."

Fine. A girl with no inhibitions, with the body and the mind for it, with the fire and desire.

Tires hummed on Wilshire and a radio played in the next unit. Her body was smooth and her artist's hands strong, her body was firm and active and finally calm.

I heard the shower above the hum of the tires but below the blare of the radio next door. I lay on my side on the double bed, at peace with the world.

Ranch-type furniture, with the insignia of the motel branded into the chairs, the bedstead, the dresser, the end tables. Western living, under the neon sign. Navajo rugs and Western prints and charcoal-broiled steaks in the grille. Howdy, podner, we even got television.

The shower hiss stopped, and Sally called, "Would you get my back, Champ?"

I went in to scrub her back.

We went from there to the Coast Highway and drove out that past Malibu, soaking up the February sun. Coming back, she parked where there was a view of the ocean, just south of where Sunset ends.

Sea gulls walked the beach below us and a few bathers lay on the sand beneath the ledge.

I told her about Sam Wald's visit the night before, and added, "It's been bothering me. He knows Max and I left with the girl, and he must have found out from the hotel clerk that Max came home alone."

"If he knows, the police know," Sally said, "and you wouldn't be sitting here if the police knew. Wald was guessing."

"I don't think so. If he was going to guess, he'd guess the other way, that Max went home with the girl."

"When you were making the play for her at the party?"

"I don't know that I was. And how do you know?"

"By the way Max told the story. Who else was at the party?"

"I don't know."

"We'll ask Max."

"Why?"

"Maybe we can learn something."

I smiled at her. "Something the police can't?"

"That's not so silly. The kind of people Max knows don't usually confide in the police, even when they've nothing to hide. We might be able to confide in the police for them."

"A couple of stool pigeons?"

"Don't be adolescent. Luke, I want to know now. Don't you?"

"I always did. And if I should learn I had committed murder, I'd want the police to know." I studied her. "Would you?"

"We'll never learn that," she said. "Not about you, Luke."

"I wish I could keep up with your moods," I said. "Fifteen hours ago, you were ready to cut my throat."

Her hand came out to rest on mine. "I know. Keep you jumping, don't I? But I do love you, Luke."

"There's another motel, right up the road a way here," I said.

She brought the left hand all the way over from her side of the car. It was a clenched hand, a fist, and it caught me right under the eye.

"You're so damned insensitive," she said. She rubbed her knuckles. "You hurt me."

My cheek throbbed, and I knew it would puff right below the eye. I said nothing, and didn't look at her, playing the strong, silent hero, wounded to the quick, wherever that is.

"Luke—" Her voice was soft, and the hand on mine was stroking my wrist. "Luke, honey, I'm sorry. I—"

Nothing from me.

"Luke, tell me what you're thinking, please."

"I'm hungry," I said. "I want a hot fudge."

"I'd rather have a drink," she said. "I know a place, not too far from here."

I looked at her suspiciously, but her face was innocent enough. "You're driving," I said. "Let's go."

She took the Coast Highway to Olympic, and Olympic to Lincoln. Lincoln is as ugly a boulevard as you'll see in any town, a truck-infested, traffic-busy thoroughfare lined with secondhand car lots, junk yards, clip joints, and all the small-shop rackets Los Angeles is loaded with, from pottery to prune juice.

Just this side of Venice, she pulled the convertible into a five-car parking-lot, next to a grimy brick building. The neon sign on top of the dump read: *Harry's Hoot Owl Club.*

"Is this the best you can do?" I asked her.

"This," she said, "is where Mary Kostanic first gained prominence in Los Angeles—sporting circles. Don't you read the *Mirror?*"

"Not if I can help it. What's on your mind?"

"A hot-fudge sundae. They're famous for them."

"It's no place for a decent girl."

"If it's good enough for Mary Kostanic, it's good enough for me. Are you frightened, Champ?"

"For you. Not for me. Some guy gets wise, and I'll be obliged to pop him, and—" I shrugged.

She climbed out of the car. "Well, then, I'll go in alone."

We went in together.

Coming from the brightness of the street, it was like a dungeon. Four booths and a bar, a mangy-looking stuffed owl returning my stare from a pedestal atop the back bar mirror. Two workingmen drank beer in the rear booth; a girl sat at the far end of the bar, reading a *Racing Form.*

Her eyes studied me appraisingly a moment, shifted to Sally, and returned to the *Form.*

The man behind the bar wasn't much bigger than Carnera. He wore a nearly white shirt and a black bow tie and a few ring scars.

Both his hamlike hands were on top of the bar, and his gaze was steady on mine. "Well, Champ! Slumming?"

Somewhere, I'd seen him before. But whether as friend or foe or neither, I couldn't recall.

"Dropped in for a drink," I said. "Haven't we met before?"

"At Stillman's," he said, "in '46. Before my fight with Burke."

"Harry Bevilaqua," I said, and held out my hand.

A smile distorted his huge face as he gripped me up to the elbow.

"This is Sally Forester, Harry," I said. "My girl."

Sally nodded and smiled. "You were a heavyweight, I'll bet."

He threw back his head and laughed. The bar shook, the windows rattled and the truck traffic right outside the door was blanketed by the blast of his mirth.

He could laugh. After what Burke had done to him. Burke had battered him into a lumpy, bloody mountain of smashed flesh, though he hadn't put him down. Burke had done everything but subdivide him.

Sally started to laugh, too, after a second, and I managed a smile. Remembering the Burke fight, the smile was a chore.

I said, "What ever happened to Burke?"

"Selling roofing, in Milwaukee. Burke would have gone some place, if he had a punch, you know that? Clever kid, but no punch."

"I never watched him much," I said. "You sound happy though, Harry."

"Punchy," he explained. "These days, that's a big help." And he laughed again, though not as loud. "Beer, Champ? A small beer? Or champagne, on the house? And the little lady, maybe a Martini? You looked good, those last couple rounds against Charley. You were kind of rough on him, though. You usually aren't so rough with Charley, are you? Friend of yours, isn't he?"

"A small beer for me will be all right," I said. "I don't know about Sally."

"Who knows about women, huh, Champ? How about Giani?"

"How about Burke?" I answered.

He laughed. "Yeh. Feather puncher, though. I'm an easy bleeder, Champ. What'll it be, Miss Sally?" He was drawing a short beer.

"Oh—champagne," Sally said. "Did you know Mary Kostanic very well, Harry?"

The girl at the far curve of the bar looked up quickly, saw my eyes on her, and dropped her gaze to the *Form*. Harry studied the collar on my beer, still under the tap. The sound of the trucks was suddenly louder in the quiet room.

Harry continued to look at the beer. "Who?"

"Mary Kostanic. Brenda Vane."

Harry set the beer carefully on the bar, his eyes never wavering from it. "I knew her well, very well. Mary liked fighters. And marines and thugs and even some cops. Tough guys, Mary liked." He looked up, and straight at Sally. "I liked Mary. I liked her a lot. She was kind of a strange girl, but we're all queer enough."

"How was she strange, Harry?" Sally's voice was gentle.

"Why? Why do you want to know?"

"Not because I'm nosy or catty," Sally said. "Not for any nasty reasons, Harry."

He looked at her for seconds. "Yuh." He took a breath, and glanced down toward the girl at the far end. "What'll you have to drink? Oh, you wanted champagne, I remember."

He reached into a refrigerated cabinet, took out a bottle, and started to peel the foil. His eyes were on the wall behind us. ¡

"The law was here. The nosy newspaper knuckle-heads were here. Even a stinking sob sister. I told 'em Mary was a clean kid with lots of talent looking for a break in a rough town. That's what the papers like, anyway." He reached for a corkscrew and began to turn it into the cork.

"Well, maybe none of it was true. The way she was strange, I got the idea she *liked* being kicked around. You know, there's people like that. Remember, Champ, that Arty Retard?"

"I remember," I said. "There's a name for the type."

"Masochist," Sally said. "They live to suffer."

Harry shrugged. He had removed the corkscrew and was working the cork out with a thumb the size of a fifty-cent cigar.

There was a *pop* and the cork went over our shoulders to bounce on the floor.

"Real good vintage," Harry said. "1952. Hah!" He winked at me. "How about Giani?"

"Is he one of your relatives? Why worry about him?"

"I don't, Champ." His big frame shook in a chuckle. "*I* won't be fighting him. Good boy, right?"

"That's what I hear. That's his claim, anyway."

Harry nodded. "Sure. Cocky. All the real brawlers are cocky. Bad boys, too, all of 'em."

He poured the champagne into a glass, and brought out another for himself. Then he lifted his in a toast.

"To better days," he said.

"And honest refs," I said.

"And real friends," Sally said.

Behind us, the door opened, and I glanced that way. I made out the peaked cap of a cab driver and then he was fully into the room and he saw me.

He stopped short and stared. He looked pale, suddenly, and then his eyes slid off me and went questioningly to Harry.

Harry's voice was too calm. "Nobody called for a cab, that I know of." He looked toward the two men in the booth. "Either of you gents call for a cab?"

To my knowledge, I'd never seen the man before. But the atmosphere was too charged for me to let this go by. I said, "Hello. Haven't seen you for two days. Come on over and have a drink."

Chapter V

HE WAS A SMALL MAN, no more than a bantam. He looked at me without recognition, and then said, "Never turn down a drink, Mac. But what's this about two days?" He came slowly over to the bar.

I said, "Didn't you carry me the other night?"

The man looked at Harry. "Whisky." And then at me. "I get a lot of fares, mister."

"From the Palisades, late, night before last?"

He shook his head. He looked at me blankly and said, "You could check the trip tickets. Haven't been out there for a week."

Harry, pouring the whisky, said, "Leave it lay, Champ. I think I know what you're talking about."

"Well, I sure as hell don't," the small man said. There was a touch of belligerence in his tone.

"Simmer down, Noodles," Harry said. "Have a drink." Then he smiled at me. "I know a couple of the boys was at the party, Champ. I get a word here and there. Relax. Have another beer."

Sally said, "Then you *did* have him in your cab, but didn't make an official record of it. Why?"

Harry stared at her blankly. "Miss Sally, you've got everything mixed up. I don't follow you at all."

Sally's chin was out again. "Exactly how stupid do you think we are?"

Harry spread both hands palm upward, like a praying oak tree. "Ma'am, what's going on? What're you getting all riled up about?"

Noodles said, "Well, I've got to be moving. Can't make any money in here. Thanks for the drink, Major."

He'd taken one step when I grabbed him by the shoulder. "Just a minute. We hadn't finished talking, Noodles."

He looked at the hand on his shoulder and up to meet my gaze. If he was frightened, he hid it well. "Take your hand off me. Who the hell you think you are?"

Harry said, "Leave him go, Champ."

"I'll fight both of you, if I have to," I said. "But my neck's involved in this business, and I don't want any brush-offs now."

Harry's big face looked sadly patient. "Champ, leave loose of him. This ain't no ring. I'm the boss and bouncer, here, and there's no ref around. Leave him go."

I tightened my grip on the little man's shoulder, and he bent in a half-crouch, a grimace of pain tightening his face.

From the corner of my eye, I saw Harry walking along toward the front, open end of the bar. I heard him coming up behind me, moving easily, and I could guess his feet were flat.

Now I could see him in the mirror at the end of the room, and I released the little man and pivoted. I brought my right hand around as I did and put every one of my hundred and sixty pounds into the button try.

I couldn't have hit him cleaner with a rifle.

I felt the shock of it all the way to my molars, and felt the bone go in my hand.

I saw the man-mountain take two backward steps and then the floor shook as he crashed a chair and toppled.

I heard Sally scream, heard a *thunk,* and turned to see Noodles going down, his knees paper, a knife gleaming in his hand.

There was a look of pure incredulity on Sally's face and a leaking champagne bottle in her hand.

My hand throbbed steadily. Noodles sat in one of the booths, his head cradled in his arms, on top of the table. Kayoed by a dame; poor Noodles would live a long time with that.

The mountain of meat known as Harry Bevilaqua sat in a chair near the booth that held Noodles, rubbing his jaw with one ridiculous hand.

"The first time, Champ," Harry said sadly. "First time I ever took a full count. And from a lousy middle—" He shook his big head.

The girl reading the *Racing Form* was still at it, working with a pencil and a scratch pad now. The two men had left.

My hand was swelling, turning blue along a streak between the middle knuckles. I said, "What do we know now?"

Harry looked at Noodles, and at the girl. He said to her, "Your nose is shiny, Ruth. You go and powder your nose. Take a lot of time; get it right."

She went out through a door at the rear of the room.

Harry glanced again at Noodles, and then looked down at his big hands. "Well, that night, Mary called about one, said a man had passed out in her place, and was there someone around that could help? Noodles was around; he went up there. Take it away, Noodles."

He shook his head, cradled in the thin arms. "To hell with them. Get the cops. To hell with them."

"Noodles," Harry said softly, "the champ is all right. That ain't only my word; you could ask any of 'em from back where it's civilized and they'll tell you Luke Pilgrim is aces. We didn't do right, playing cute with him. The lady's sorry, Noodles, but you shouldn't have pulled no knife on the champ."

The little man shivered and lifted his head. He glared at me. "You were up there, outside, sitting on the curb. I picked you up and brought you back to the hotel. And now that I told you, it'll be all right if I tell the cops, huh, Cheese Champ?"

"Noodles," Harry said, "Luke's no cheese champ. You saw that right he hit me with. Or did you?"

"I didn't see nothing," Noodles said. "But I will, and I want a ringside seat when Giani beats his brains out."

"That we'll see," Harry said. "But *cops*, Noodles, what kind of people call copper? Not our kind of people."

Sally said, "I'm sorry I hit you, Mr. Noodles, but I love Luke and you were going to kill him. Wouldn't you want your girl to do as much for you?"

"I ain't got a girl," he said. "Lay off me."

I said, "For Christ's sake, if you want to scream for the law, there's the phone. But quit whimpering. You boys may as well know I blanked out from the seventh round until breakfast the next morning. I learned later, from Max, about the party and about taking the redhead— Mary Kostanic home. Or rather, going home with her. I want to know what happened, too, damn you. *I want to know if I'm a murderer.*"

Silence, while both of them stared at me.

Sally said, "That wasn't very bright, Luke. Only you and Max and I knew about the blackout, until now."

"They can take it to the law," I told her, "and then try to explain why they've been so quiet about their part in it. They could take years to explain that away."

"It still wasn't very bright," Sally said.

"Neither am I. Well, boys?"

Harry looked thoughtfully at Noodles. Noodles still stared at me.

Then Harry smiled. "We ain't mad no more, huh,

Noodles?"

Noodles shrugged. A flicker of cunning crossed his thin face.

Harry said, "Was it that high right hand, in the seventh, Champ? Was that what put you in the black?"

"That was it." I continued to look at the little cabbie. "Was Mary alive when you picked me up at the curb?"

"I don't know. That's straight. There was a light on up there, but nothing moving, so I don't know."

"That's no help," I said. "Do you remember a bakery sign on the supermarket at the top of the hill above that Conference Grounds. It's a Mayfair Market."

"Bakery sign?" Noodles frowned. "You mean one of them windmills?"

"That's right. What happened there?"

"You got me. Nothing."

"Did you come into the hotel with me?"

He shook his head. "You gave me a ten and told me to keep the change, and I took off."

"I was drunk?"

"No, I don't think so. You didn't weave any. You seemed kind of—oh, hell—punchy, I guess."

Sally said, "You probably walked right past the clerk at the desk. Luke, your hand—"

"Yup," I said. "Bone broken, I'm sure."

"Geez," Harry said. "Champ, you standing there and that hand—That's your living, man—You'd better—"

"I'll be going in a minute," I said. "Noodles, whether you like me or not, I'd appreciate everything you can tell me. You won't have to go to the law, if I killed her. I will."

"That's all I know," Noodles said. "So help me, that's every word of it."

"Sally," I said, "phone Max at the hotel. Tell him to have a doctor there. He'll know a good one. I don't want just any doctor on this hand. We'd better go; it's getting bad."

Harry said, "You should have hit me with a bottle or a chair, Champ. Christ, that's—" He was chewing his full lower lip.

"I'll drop in again," I said. "I've got to get some air."

The floor wavered a little, but I made the sunlight and felt better. I stood next to the doorway, sucking in the warm air, trying to concentrate on not getting sick.

Then Sally came out, the keys in her hand. "Max will have a doctor there. Let's go. You're all right, Luke?"

"It feels worse than it is," I said, "but don't lose any time."

She made the flivver talk, and they talk very well for their size and weight. We got to the hotel a few minutes before the doctor.

Max met us at the door, his face stormy. "What in the hell kind of mess is this, now?" He didn't look at Sally.

Neither of us answered him. I sat in the big chair near the window; Sally went to get me a drink of water.

"Brawling," Max said, "like some slap-happy bum. What came over you?"

"Self-defense, Max," I said. "Remember Harry Bevilaqua?"

"I think. Freak—big freak? Nobody ever put him away, though."

"I just did. And I learned how I got back from the redhead's."

"How?"

"Cab. The girl phoned Harry for help, and he sent a cabbie up. Maybe he came in his car instead of a cab; I didn't check that. Anyhow, *she* phoned."

"Then she was alive when you left her."

"The cabbie doesn't know. I was waiting outside."

"That's great. And why didn't he go to the law?"

I stared at Max. Sally brought my water and held it

for me to sip, and I couldn't get my mind from Max's words. Why hadn't Noodles gone to the law? Not because of any love for me; on that I'd give odds.

The doctor came, and I got the hypo, right off. There was no broken bone but a strained muscle; nothing permanent. So far as he could tell now.

He left, and Max said, "Well, if it's not too much trouble, I'd like to hear the story that goes with the hand."

I told him about it and all the time I talked I was thinking of his remark about Noodles.

The relief the hypo brought relaxed me, and I dozed off, the sound of tires soothing. Windmills came tilting at me and the big woman in white shorts danced a tango with Max. *"Died, died, died"*—someone said.

It was Sally, and I opened my eyes.

"Where the hell you been?" Max was saying. "It was on all the radio stations."

Sally was crying. "That nice man, that decent, sweet, dignified, courageous—"

"Who?" I asked. "Who died, Sally?"

"King George," Max answered me. "And look at her. She never even saw him."

"I never did, either," I said, "but I know how she feels."

I felt a little that way, myself. I'm not as sentimental as Sally, but in today's world, a gentleman sure as hell stands out by contrast. A quiet, mannerly man, dying inside and knowing it, carrying on in the gentle tradition, holding an empire together by the decency he symbolized.

In a world where the loudest liars got the most ink it was nice to know a *gentleman's* death didn't go unnoticed.

It was late afternoon and the hum of westbound traffic was steady. Max played solitaire, Sally read, and I thought of Noodles, that tough little guy.

There were things he knew and hadn't told me, I'd bet. But there wasn't anything he knew he'd tell before he was damned good and ready. He wasn't the kind of cookie you could beat anything out of.

Harry could get him to talk, but it hadn't been with threats or muscle.

Sally looked up from her book. "What are you thinking of?"

"Noodles."

"Me, too. We ought to go back and see him again."

Max looked up from his solitaire game. "Over my dead body."

"That could be arranged," Sally said, not looking at him. "Luke, didn't you get the feeling Noodles was lying?"

"No, not exactly that. I got the feeling there was something he knew and was careful about not telling us."

"That's lying, isn't it? In my book, that's lying."

"You read the wrong books. He doesn't have to tell us anything; we're not the law."

"Right," Max cut in with. "You're two-hundred-per-cent right, Mr. Pilgrim. And one way to get into trouble is to act like the law when you're not."

Now Sally looked at him. "Or lie to them, like *you* did."

Max returned her stare. "It seemed like a good time for a lie. Or would you rather see your lovey-dovey in a gas chamber?"

"Luke's innocent," she said. "I know it, now. And they don't execute innocent people, not in America."

"Huh!" Max said. "You're the innocent one. What a statement. You talk like a Girl Scout."

"I was a Girl Scout. There's something wrong with that, Mr. Freeman?"

"Huh!" Max said, and went back to the solitaire.

"Great conversationalist, isn't he?" Sally asked me. "When he hasn't an answer, he says 'huh.' Never at a loss for a 'huh.' No wonder you're both broke, with Max doing the thinking."

Now Max looked really annoyed. He said, "We haven't any written contract, me and Luke. He's free, any damned time he wants to leave me. Maybe under your management he could do better. I here and now give him to you." He stood up. "I'm moving out."

"Sit down," I said, and looked at Sally. "And you shut up. You're acting like an idiot. Both of you are."

"I'm going down for a drink, then," Max said. "I won't move out until she moves in." He looked at Sally. "I mean—moves her clothes in; she's already taken over everything else."

"Max," I said, "I love you, but you haven't got her build. Why don't we make up and all go down for a drink?"

"Not today," Max said. "Maybe tomorrow, but not today." He went out, and the door slammed behind him.

Sally pretended to read.

I said, "Why don't you get out of his hair?"

"Why doesn't he get out of mine? He's jealous, I think. Could that be?"

"No. If you want a drink, order one. And a bottle of beer for me, Eastern beer."

"Yes, dear," she said. "Aren't we bossy, though? Aren't we the executive type?"

"My hand hurts," I told her, "and you two sit there and bicker like a couple of punks. Why don't you read to me?"

"This one's beyond you," she said. "I'll order the drinks and we'll talk."

Scotch, she had, and the boy brought me a bottle of Milwaukee beer. We talked about marriage, and where would we live?

"Here?" I suggested.

"I don't know. So many phonies. It's got everything, Luke, but it's so—transient, sort of."

"Four million people in the county," I said. "Some of them are bound to be real. I like it, phonies and all."

"And what would you do?"

"I don't know. Live off you. This should be a good town for a commercial artist."

"It isn't. I'd live off you, and how much can you make, selling pencils?"

"I could write a sports column, or something. That should be a breeze, in this town. Or I could fight Patsy Giani and bet all the money I could borrow plus my share of the purse on him."

"You've ducked him long enough. I wonder why the Commission lets Max get away with that?"

"Nobody decent wants Patsy Giani as a champ. Nobody who has any regard for boxing."

"Giani," she said thoughtfully. "And Bevilaqua. Both Italian, aren't they?"

"Mmmm-hmmm. But if you think there's a connection, you're wrong. Harry hates the man's guts, though he admires his power."

"He didn't sound that way to me."

"It isn't how he sounds, it's how he is. Harry had a lot of regard for the boxing game, and he probably still has. His manager was one of the straightest noodles in the business."

"You're certainly a fast man with an opinion. There's something back in that owl's roost that we didn't get. I can feel it; I know it. We ought to go back."

"After my hand's better. I'd be at a disadvantage there, with only the left hand."

"Did you see that girl at the end of the bar? Do you think she was—a—you know—a—"

"I don't know. I'll find out when we go back. Don't be so superior, my motel miss."

"You're vulgar," she said. "That's just one of the reasons I'm afraid to marry you. You're cruel, at times, and vulgar a lot, and you haven't any money sense at all. And you're not very well read."

"Think of my body and forget the rest. Not an ounce of fat on me. Did you see me tip over that big dago?"

"Italian. That's another thing, you're bigoted."

"No. I'm sorry; I was trying to annoy you. You know I'm not bigoted."

"All right, then, not that. But vulgar and occasionally cruel and highly opinionated and egotistical, too. You think you're something."

"I am," I said. "I'm champ."

"Champ! In what kind of trade?"

"In my trade. Remember, we talked about King George, and that's what I liked about him. He was champ in his trade."

"Edward would have been better."

"No. He had his chance at the title, and missed it. Never mind why; he wasn't man enough for the job. But George was."

"Edward gave up the crown for the woman he loved. Wouldn't you?"

"No. I wouldn't give it up for Jesus Christ. I earned it; the next champ is going to have to take it away from me. The man ahead of me went out on his back, and I put him there. The one who follows me will have to be as good."

"And you want to choose your successor?" Her smile was impudent. "You'll fight some more bums. Patsy Giani will never get the chance *you* got, will he?"

"That's up to Max."

"You wouldn't be afraid of him?"

"I'm not afraid of anybody in the world."

"You probably aren't," she said. "You're too damned dumb to be scared of anything. You haven't the necessary imagination."

"Come on over and sit in my lap. Let's make up."

"You go to hell. I hate you when you're so—realistic and certain and pseudo-logical."

"Let's play canasta."

"No, I want to read. I'm all talked out and I don't like canasta."

"We could lock the door," I said, "and—"

"Shut up. I want to read."

She read. Tires hummed. My hand throbbed. I saw Harry Bevilaqua crash and heard Noodles whimper and saw the maroon sheets and the big woman in shorts. Busy little bees, we'd been, gayly investigating this B girl's death.

Mary Kostanic, known professionally as Brenda Vane, liked tough guys. And was I a tough guy? I suppose to her I was. To a lot of people I am. But I really never left All Saints.

Murder is a word used too easily. *Murder the bum . . . I'm telling you it was murder . . . That gown is simply murderous, Mrs. Vere de Vere . . .*

Murder is more important than that; it's a double death, killing the killer as well as the killed, ending the dream and staining the soul. The newspapers love it, especially if one breast or more can be exposed, along with the inside of the thigh.

That makes a good picture, and who's got time to read? With wrestling on the television, who's got time to read about why Brenda Vane died? Who cares? *She couldn't a'been much; ya ever seen 'er in pitchers? Or on television?*

Sally turned a page and the twin tail pipes of a hot rod made music on Sunset.

I thought of Sergeant Sands, the gray-black hair, the knowing blue eyes, the free and steady and easy way he moved around this case. That was no prelim boy, that Sergeant Sands.

Somebody laughed in the hall, and Sally turned a page. I went out to the patio and got the Hemingway. I came in and stretched out on the davenport with it.

Max came in with an afternoon paper, and went through to the patio. He turned on the little radio, out there; Max can't take his reading straight. He dilutes it with music.

Sally looked up, frowning. I smiled.

Someone knocked at the door.

Max called, "I'll get it. It's for me, I'm sure. One of the local reporters wants an interview, Champ."

He opened the door, but it wasn't a reporter. It was the slim, blasé character, the smoothie in the blue flannel, the desk clerk.

"I wonder if you gentlemen have a little time right now?" he asked.

Chapter VI

MAX SAID, "You've got nothing to sell, skinny. You already sold it to Sam Wald."

"Wald?" the clerk said. "I don't know any Wald."

"Let him come in, Max," I said. "You're blocking the door."

"To hell with him," Max said. "Let him squeak to the law."

Sally said, "For heaven's sake, Max, go back to your comic page. Luke and I will handle this."

Max turned to look at her, and then his gaze shifted to me.

"I'd like to talk to him, Max," I said. "Maybe he just wants my autograph."

Max took a deep breath and went back to the patio.

The smoothie smiled and came in, closing the door behind him.

"What's your name?" I asked him. I wore my tough-guy look.

"It doesn't matter. You know who I am."

"All right. What do you want?"

"I was thinking you might need a witness." He'd come over to stand near the davenport, where I was still stretched out.

He didn't look as though my tough-guy front was getting to him one bit.

"Witness?" I said.

Sally said, "Won't you sit down, Mr.—"

"No, thanks. I won't be here long." He didn't look at her. "I mean, if you should get called into court on this Brenda Vane case, you might need me as a witness to prove you came in the same time your manager did, that night."

"Oh. And—"

"Well, witness fees aren't much. It wouldn't pay me to take off from my job."

"I see. But you've already told the police you don't remember my coming in with my manager."

"Not under oath, I didn't."

Sally cut into the momentary silence. "What did you figure would be a reasonable witness fee?"

Now he turned to look at her. "I thought you people could set a price. You'd know what it's worth to you."

I laughed, and he colored. I asked, "First time? Is this your first journey into the criminal world, cutie?"

His jaw was rigid, while color flooded his face. "I don't see anything funny."

"Get him a mirror, Sally," I said. "The nameless terror. Do you realize, punk, that this is one of the better suites in this rattrap? Do you realize you'd be out of a job right now, if I should pick up that phone and call the manager? Run along, boy, somebody might want some ice water."

His color had left, now, and his face was grimly pale. Not fear, but anger and hate. "You're a fighter, and I don't scare you. I'll tell you something, Mr. Pilgrim, you don't scare me, either. And you're going to be damned sorry you talked to me the way you did."

"I suppose," I said. "But that's life, Killer."

I was talking to his back. The door slammed behind him as I got to the last word.

"You fool," Sally said. "You muscle-bound loud mouth."

"I did something wrong?"

"Couldn't you have used a little finesse? Did you have to humiliate him? Is it necessary to make an enemy of him?"

"You always liked those smooth and superior knot-heads," I told her. "Those slim and well-tailored mealy mouths can always get to you, can't they?"

The book she threw missed me by a foot.

"Let's not fight," I said. "Let's neck."

She sat forward in her chair, looking like the challenger on his stool. "Luke, that was absolutely brainless. He *can* go to Sergeant Sands, you know. This *is* a murder case."

"He can," I agreed, "but why should he? He won't make a dollar there. Maybe, from somebody else, he could get a dollar or two for the information, somebody like— oh, Sam Wald."

"Oh? Hasn't he told Wald already?"

"I don't think so. I think Sam got his information somewhere else. Or was guessing. This punk isn't that dumb, trying to sell both sides."

"And you want him to go to Wald?"

"Mmmm-hmmm."

"Why?"

"So he can put the heat to me for the Giani fight. So Patsy can think I'm afraid of him, that I wouldn't fight him unless I was forced into it. Might give him the wrong mental approach to the fight. And a good slap on the chops might throw all his planning off. Is that clear?"

"No."

"I mean, he might not expect me to take the offensive, and when I do, he might not be ready for it."

She shook her head. "Nobody thinks you can beat Giani, not Max, nor that big Harry, nor Sergeant Sands nor any sports writer I've read. Why should you?"

"I don't. But I've got to fight him anyway, and I might

as well use all the weapons I can."

"You couldn't retire undefeated, I suppose? You've got to prove something to yourself."

"I suppose. Let's not talk about it." I stood up and went to the phone. I asked the operator, "Would you get me the west-side station of the Los Angeles Police Department, please?"

I could feel Sally's eyes on me. I could hear Max's feet on the concrete of the patio and then I could see him standing in the entrance way.

I said, "Could I speak with Sergeant Sands, please? This is Luke Pilgrim."

Sands wasn't there. Would another officer do?

"If his partner's there," I said. "I think it's that big redhead." Just a hunch I was playing.

The redhead was there, Sergeant Nolan, and I said, "I don't know if you're familiar with my part in the Brenda Vane case, but the night clerk at the hotel here has just attempted to blackmail me in connection with it. I thought you might want to know about it."

"Blackmail you, Mr. Pilgrim? How?"

"He wanted me to pay him for swearing I came home with my manager that night Miss Vane was killed."

"There weren't any witnesses to the attempt, I suppose?"

"Two, though they're both friends of mine."

"I see. How clearly did the clerk word his demand?"

"I think I could give it to you almost word for word. I've a pretty good memory."

"I see. Well, Mr. Pilgrim, I'll talk to Sergeant Sands about it. He'll undoubtedly want a statement from all three of you. He'll get in touch with you."

"Thank you," I said, and hung up.

Sally shook her head. Max looked at me doubtfully.

I said, "I suppose it never occurred to either of you

that Sergeant Sands, himself, might have sent that clerk here just to get a reaction?"

"Nonsense," Sally said.

"Nuts," Max said.

"Besides," I told them, "I'm not a defensive fighter. I think it's time we went on the offense. After all, I *might* be innocent." I went back to the davenport. "How did you like that for finesse, Mrs. Forester? Smooth, eh?"

"Your brains are scrambled," Max said.

Sally looked at him. "Maxie, honey, we've finally found an area of agreement, as they say. Are we friends, Max?"

"Aaahh," he said, and went back to his patio.

"I'll be friends with you, Sal," I said.

"Aaahh," she said, and came over to pick up the book she'd thrown.

My hand was still sore, but there wasn't any more throb. I held it up and looked at it, my good right hand that would be good again, I hoped. Good enough for Patsy Giani, I hoped.

"Boom, boom," I said, "and there goes Patsy."

Sally turned a page.

"Whammo," I said. "That old man Pilgrim still has a wallop. Look at Patsy reel around the ring. Migawd, he's covered with blood. He's out on his feet. He's—"

"Will you please be quiet?" Sally asked. "*I am trying to read.*"

"How can you read with the battle of the century going on? Giani's down. He's trying to get up. Oh, folks, this is an awful sight, this young man, bleeding from the mouth and over both eyes, trying to get up, to strike back at this terrible ring tiger, this inhuman master of the most brutal of the arts, this sneering, cold perfectionist who has, round by round—"

"*Shut up!*" Sally said.

"Okay, okay. Spoilsport."

I arched my back, stretched my legs, and considered the ceiling. Start with the windmill; what does the wind-mill mean, what is it trying to tell you? It is a Dutch wind-mill and—wait, Dutch Krueger is Giani's manager— No, start over. It is the trade-mark of a baker and I knew a promoter in Houston named Baker who— No.

Chimes sounded.

"That's the door," I told Sally. "Answer it, will you?" She glared at me.

"My hand hurts," I said. "I'm afraid if I try to get up, I—"

"I'll get it," Max said. "It's probably that newspaper guy." He came through from the patio as the chimes sounded again.

It was no newspaper guy. It was three men. One of them was Sam Wald, one of them was a dark, bald man over six feet high and looking almost that broad. The third man could have been related to Noodles; he had the same general build. Only he was tougher, or wanted you to think he was, at any rate. I'd have backed Noodles, with my money.

"What the hell is this?" Max asked. They'd come in without an invitation.

"We wanted to talk to you, Max," Sam said. "Big-money talk, Max. We knew you'd be interested in that." His insurance-salesman smile was working. "This is Paul D'Amico, Max. And Luke Pilgrim, Paul."

Big man, out here, Paul D'Amico. Back East, pretty big, too. But out here, Mr. Big.

"Who's the little guy?" I asked. I didn't get up.

The little man's fish eyes looked me over without emo-tion. Then he looked at D'Amico and shrugged.

"Haven't I seen him in pictures? I see a lot of B pic-tures."

The little man went over to stand near the door.

I looked over to find Sally staring at me with fright in her eyes. I winked at her, and shook my head.

Max said, "We got nothing to talk about, Sam. I told you that. You got a kick, go to the Commission. Pull any strings you want. But, for Christ's sake, don't try to muscle me. I got too many friends."

The little guy leaned against the door, his hands behind him, his disinterested gaze going out straight at nothing. He fascinated me. He could have been John Doe, except for the eyes.

D'Amico said, "Don't get riled, Max. You're not that solvent. And you're not getting half out of the title that a smart man would get. There could be millions in it."

Sally said, "I'm going to my room, Luke. I'll phone you later."

She got up, looking sick, and took three steps to the door. The little man didn't move anything but his head. His head was turned toward D'Amico, waiting for the *word*.

D'Amico wasn't looking at him and it wasn't intentional, I'm sure. But the redness grew in me, the unreasonable, wild redness. I got up, and swung my feet to the floor.

I said hoarsely, "Get that God-damned pimp away from the door or I'll rip his spine out."

Just a flicker in the fish eyes, but a startled turn of the head from D'Amico and he said, "Johnny—move!"

Johnny moved, and Sally went through.

D'Amico looked back at me. "It wasn't intentional, Luke. What in the hell's the matter with you guys?"

I was trembling. The throbbing was back in my hand and sweat ran down my forearms. The fish eyes regarded me gravely. Wald coughed.

Then Wald said, "What happened to your hand, Luke?"

I sat back on the davenport, my heart hammering. Cool, calm Luke Pilgrim, always under control. Oh, yes.

Max said, "What the hell have we got to talk about? You come in here without being asked, bringing your torpedo along and start throwing your weight around. The Champ's had enough trouble the last couple days without this kind of crap. Where the hell do you think you are, Cicero?"

Wald said, "I apologize for coming in. I didn't think our relationship was that formal, Max."

"Since when are we related?" Max asked.

D'Amico laughed. Even I had to laugh. Wald smiled, and Johnny yawned.

D'Amico said, "Johnny's no torpedo, Max. He's just an old friend. If you want, I'll have him wait in the lobby. Sam brought me here because I have the controlling interest in Patsy Giani, and can bring the kind of promotion to the fight that'll make us all a barrel of money."

"I'm not interested," Max said.

"I am," I said. "I like money. Sit down, gentlemen."

Wald smiled. D'Amico asked, "Johnny, too?"

"Absolutely," I said. "The type fascinates me. I like to watch him."

The pint-sized killer went over to sit on the chair near the telephone, a straight, uncomfortable chair. Maybe, if Max didn't have so many friends, Johnny would have scared me. But Max had friends at all the levels, from municipal to federal and Johnny, I'm sure, was a pro. Johnny was no trigger-happy punk; he'd know how many strings Max Freeman had out.

And without his gun, what was Johnny?

Max was watching me coldly, and I could guess he was thinking of walking out on the whole deal. But habit was strong, with Max, and I was still his boy. He sat down near me on the davenport.

Wald took the chair Sally had occupied; D'Amico sat in its twin on the other side of the tier table.

"All right," I said. "Start talking about money."

Light glistened off Paul D'Amico's bald head, a reflection from the diamond on Max's little finger. D'Amico looked at Wald.

Wald said, "The kind of money we could talk about might seem ridiculous. It would depend, of course, on how well the fight was built up, and how much money was wagered. In a town where *wrestling* gets sports-page space, ink should be cheap. On the betting, of course, we could build it to five to six and take your choice. It would shape up, in the public's mind, to that even a match, I'm sure. With the money spread right, five to six makes the handler a certain and predetermined profit, no matter who wins." He took a breath. "That's honest enough, isn't it?"

He'd said "of course" twice, "I'm sure" once and "certain" once. Nothing doubtful in Sam's careful mind.

Wald smiled, Max glowered, D'Amico watched me shrewdly, and Johnny considered the air in the middle of the room.

"Sounds very interesting," I said. "I don't know about this hand, though. It might not be ready for some time."

"There's no hurry," D'Amico said easily.

"It might never be ready," I said.

Silence, while they studied me, all but Johnny. All but Johnny looked puzzled, too.

I said, "But the public wouldn't need to know how bad the hand was. It might affect the odds."

Wald smiled. D'Amico smiled. Max said, "What the hell are you saying, Luke?"

"I'm not getting any younger, Max. Or richer."

Max said quietly, "If you're saying what I think you're saying, this is the end of us, Luke. And I'll go to the Association with it."

Johnny's gaze came back from the middle of nowhere to fasten on Max. Wald and D'Amico looked at Max.

"Sure you could, Max," I said. "And I might wind up in the gas chamber. Is that right, gentlemen?"

Wald said nothing. D'Amico's big shoulders shrugged. "Who knows? I didn't say it."

"No. Nobody said it. But it's been in the room. You didn't really need Johnny, not for this trip, did you?"

D'Amico shrugged again. "I don't like rough talk. That's mug stuff. We don't need it at this level."

"That's right. And I don't like to do anything without Max. I never have. We can talk again, can't we?"

Both of them glanced at Max, and back at me. "Sure," D'Amico said, and stood up. "You call us, or we'll drop in. Whatever you want."

"I'll let you know," I said, and smiled.

Wald stood up. Johnny stood up. Max still sat. I walked to the door with them.

I asked, "How about Johnny? Doesn't he ever talk?"

D'Amico smiled at him. "Great little guy. One of the very best. Hell, yes, he can talk loud when he wants to. Got a great big voice when he needs it. Just doesn't use words."

Silence in the room when they left. Max sat on the davenport, staring into space, when I turned from the door.

I went over to the phone and called Sally's room. I said, "They're gone. Let's go out and eat. It's about that time."

"I'll be over," she said.

I put the phone back into the cradle and turned to face Max. He still wouldn't look at me.

"They don't scare me," I said. "Giani doesn't scare me."

"Who said they did? You gave them the idea you'd sell out. You weren't planning to cross them, were you?"

"Sure. That's what I meant when I said they don't scare me. I'd cross them, tomorrow, and spit in their eyes when they came to moan about it."

"Came to moan? You lard-head, you mean come to *mourn*, don't you? You wouldn't live long enough to spit."

"Nuts," I said. "I know the type."

"*You* know the type? From where? From the choir? From high school? Look, Luke, I grew up with the type. I've seen them operate, from twelve on. Don't get any nice ideas about what they'd do. Don't ever get the idea you could cross them and get away with it." His face softened. "Though I'd rather see you dead, at that, than what I thought you were, for a while, there."

I said, "I'm sorry, Max. You could be right, but I just can't get scared about those—freaks."

Again the chimes sounded. Grand Central Station.

Max said, "It's about time that reporter showed." He went to the door.

Sergeant Sands—and Sally. The sergeant said, "Nolan told me you phoned."

"Come in, Sergeant," I said. "There's more, now."

Max and Sally turned to look at me questioningly. I said, "I've just had a talk with Paul D'Amico."

The sergeant didn't blink an eye. He came over to sit in one of the twin chairs. "I know it. What did he want?"

"A title fight for Patsy Giani. D'Amico's got the idea he knows more about the murder than you do, and he was using the threat as a lever to get me to sign."

"Threat?"

"He seems to think I went home with Brenda Vane."

"So does the room clerk. What happened to your hand?"

"I don't know. You could ask the doctor that treated it. It was a little sore, right after the fight, but nothing like this."

"What's the doctor's name?"

Max gave it to him, and Sands wrote it down. Then he sat there quietly a moment, looking at his thumbnail.

"The fight was all D'Amico wanted?"

"He wasn't too clear, but I think he wanted a dive to go with it."

"Giani—diving?"

"No. Me."

The sergeant was frowning. "You? It doesn't add."

"Why not?"

He looked at the thumbnail again. "I hope you're not sensitive, but I told you I was a fight fan. Honestly, now, you wouldn't have a ghost of a chance with Giani in a straight fight, would you?"

"That's right," Max said. "He wouldn't."

The redness. The image of Sands wavered, then came into focus.

Sally said, "Easy, Luke, baby."

"I guess," I said, "I'm the only guy in the world who thinks I can lick Giani. Maybe my judgment's off. I meant to give D'Amico the idea I would bet on Giani. I meant to give Giani his licking, and D'Amico one hell of a financial licking. I had it all figured out, real cute."

"You were going to cross Paul D'Amico?"

"Mmmm-hmmm."

"God," Sands said. "Good Lord." It wasn't blasphemy. It was a prayer.

Max said, "That ain't all, Sergeant. He was going to pop that little torpedo of D'Amico's. He called him a pimp and offered to rip his spine out."

"Johnny?"

"That's right. The wordless wonder. The guy who never talks."

"He can't talk," Sands said. "He's a mute. If D'Amico told Johnny to cut off his hand above the wrist with an old tin can, Johnny would do it. Florida cops made Johnny a mute, ruined his vocal cords. All the cops involved died, eventually, one way or another. Johnny is a part of

D'Amico."

Max said, "And Golden Boy, here, thinks he understands people like that. He's seen a lot of gangster pictures, so he knows all about them."

Sands shook his head, studying me.

Max said, "No offense, Sergeant, but would *you* cross Paul D'Amico?"

Sands's head turned slowly, as he looked at Max. "No," he said.

Sally said, "What difference does it make? Luke would. There aren't many people in the world like Luke. You should know that by now, Max."

"The world's full of them," Max said. "Some of 'em are even dumber."

The sergeant almost smiled. He looked at me wearily. "You've been champ a long time. Certain attitudes that title gives you have hardened your conceit to a point where you think you're invulnerable. No man is. No nation is, no idea is, no form of matter is. You're a little better in your trade than the average, but D'Amico isn't in your trade. You say he doesn't scare you? You don't even *register* on him, not as a threat. He could have you destroyed tomorrow and not even use people he knew. The price would be a little higher, because of your prominence, but it wouldn't be much higher than he earns in say, oh—less than a week. What difference does it make if he scares you or not? You'd be just as dead."

Silence. Nobody said anything for seconds. Then the sergeant said, "I'll be getting along. Still got a lot of hours ahead of me. We'll get the statements about the clerk when we need them. Might never need them. I'll drop in and throw the fear of God into him tonight. No record, and we don't want to start him with one unless we have to." He stood up. "Stick to things you understand, Pilgrim, and let me know about any and all of the things that happen to you."

He stared at me, looking tired and puzzled. "Isn't there something psychologists call 'the death wish'? Maybe that's what's wrong with you."

"There's nothing wrong with him," Sally said, "except he's not afraid of a physical threat. And he's not too bright."

Another of the near smiles came to the sergeant's face. "He doesn't need to be bright, with a girl like you. Keep him out of trouble. We might need him one of these days."

He left, and Max went in to shave. I sat near the window, watching the solid stream of home-bound traffic. Sally turned on the radio.

Again, the chimes sounded.

From the bathroom, Max called, "Whoever it is, tell them to go to hell. I've had enough visitors today."

Sally went to the door, and opened it. The man there showed her something he held in his hand and said something to her too low for me to hear.

Then Sally called, "It's a reporter, Max, and he claims you promised him an interview this afternoon."

Chapter VII

MAX STAYED IN THE BATHROOM while I talked to the reporter. He wanted to know, first, about Giani.

I gave it some thought, and said, "I think he's earned his chance at the title. There's a definite possibility we'll meet this year. Maybe this spring."

"You're kidding," he said.

"Why should I be kidding?"

"I mean—well, everyone's had the feeling you were never going to fight him."

"That's silly," I said. "He just hasn't been a match until now. He hasn't been enough to make the fight profitable."

Skepticism was plain on the reporter's face. He smiled at me, saying nothing.

I said, "Look at the trouble Patsy had with Charley Retzer. And look what I did to Charley the other night."

"Retzer was younger when Giani fought him. Younger and a hell of a lot better. Or am I wrong?"

"Retzer was younger," I agreed. "Next question?"

"Champ, you've given me a beat. Now, this makes a story, this Giani bout. It's solid, it's for the record?"

"Nothing's been signed," I said, "but I'm willing, if we can make the right terms. That you can print."

"That we will," he said. "To hell with the feature story; this I've got to write." He stood up. "Thanks a lot."

"It will probably be out here," I said, "opening that

new sport bowl in the Valley."

"Oh," he said, "a Sam Wald promotion."

"I guess."

"Well, he won't need to beg for publicity on this one. It's a natural."

"That's what we figured," I said, "and this is a sports town."

When he left, Max came out of the bathroom. "Big boy, aren't you?" he asked. "You don't need me."

"I wouldn't fight without you in the corner, Max."

No answer from him.

Sally said, "We're going to eat together, aren't we? Don't sulk, Max."

"I've got to see some people," he said. "Can't make it tonight." He looked at me meaningfully. "If you intend to fight this wop, you'd better start training, if you know what I mean."

"I know what you mean," Sally said. "I'll help you on that, Max."

He went into the bedroom and Sally smirked at me. "It's a good thing I'm not sensitive. I know a place to eat."

"What kind of place?" I asked suspiciously. "Not *Harry's Hoot Owl Club?*"

"Of course not. A refined place. Let's go."

Refined was a good word for the spot; it was overrefined, a swish-mecca, a pansy bed.

Near the ocean, in Santa Monica, a place of pastel colors and soft music, of some long-haired boys and a few crew cuts who might be there only for the ride.

The food was good, and the place was restful but I'm the kind of roughneck who's annoyed by the sight of the unmanly.

"Looking for somebody special?" I asked Sally.

"Mmmm-hmmm. I phoned him this afternoon. He's going to meet us here."

"One of the—boys?"

"He wasn't when I was out here before. He's an artist turned photographer. He worked a lot with Brenda Vane. I didn't know this was one of—those places, Luke. Doesn't it give you the creeps?"

"Yup, but it's all a matter of taste, you know. Some pugs prefer this kind of company."

"Wrestlers, too, I hear."

"I was talking of the human race," I said, "not wrestlers. Why do you think your friend wanted you to meet him *here?*"

"I don't know. Here he comes now."

The gent coming toward us wore a silver-blue suit of some soft and beautifully tailored material. He had a thin, finely modeled face and startling blue eyes. His hair was white silk, long and in perfect waves.

"Sally, baby," he said, as I rose. His voice was warm.

"Hello, Michael," she said. "Michael Lord, Luke Pilgrim."

His thin-fingered hand gripped mine strongly. "I've seen you fight," he said. "You're a true champion, Mr. Pilgrim."

"Thank you," I said. "Lots of sports writers would give you an argument on that."

"No, because I wouldn't argue with a sports writer. I hear you're doing very well, Sally. I see a lot of your work in the magazines." He sat down on my side of the table.

"I make a living," Sally said. "How's the photography?"

"As a photographer," he said easily, "I was nothing much. You'll remember I wasn't much of an artist, either. However, there's another branch of the game at which I do very well."

Art studies, as they're called, I thought.

"Pornography?" Sally asked.

"A blunt word." He smiled at her. "You wanted to talk

about Brenda Vane?"

Sally nodded, studying Michael. "She posed for that sort of trash?"

"She loved it. Brenda had an overpowering compulsion to debase herself. A masochist, too, you know."

"So I've heard. You, too, Michael?"

"No. Money motivates me. I had no talent. You know I had no talent, Sally. But you did. And now you illustrate underwear advertisements. Which is the greater fall?"

"Yours. Mine sells underwear. Why did you want to meet us here, Michael?"

"I wanted to show you off to my friends, both of you. They're prestige-conscious, these lads. They model for me, too, you know. I make *all* kinds of pictures, Sally. To suit *any* taste."

Flawlessly tailored, impeccably groomed, cleanly scented, he sat there, showing us the dry rot inside him.

"Tell me about Brenda," Sally said.

I could feel the glances of the boys from time to time, as Michael Lord told Sally about Brenda. Michael's fine face glowed as he talked glibly about Brenda, as he held us spellbound for the admiration of his stooges.

He used a lot of words and told us nothing we didn't know. Until he said, "She was shacked up with Sam Wald for a while, I heard. Remember, that's just something I heard."

"That's kind of coming down the ladder for Sam Wald, isn't it?" I said. "He could do better than that."

"If you were in my business," Lord said, "you'd never be amazed at a man's taste. Brenda could offer a lot—to anybody."

Sally looked at me when he said that. Then she said, "I think we'd better hurry, Luke. The Bronsons will be waiting."

"The Bronsons" was a name we used when we wanted

to get away fast. Sally looked pale.

I paid the bill in a hurry and got her out of that refined atmosphere. Outside, she took a deep breath of air and stood quietly, looking up at the stars.

Then she said quietly, "For two weeks in the spring of 1946, I was thinking of marrying Michael Lord. Isn't he a *monster*, Luke?"

"I think he's kind of cute," I said. "Where now?"

"Underwear advertisements—he's got his nerve, the puke." She was looking out at the traffic on the street.

"Well, you do a lot of them," I said. "He's about half right on that."

She turned to glare at me. "I'm *not* gifted. I'm talented, but not gifted. Do you understand the difference between those two words?"

"I guess. Couldn't you do illustrations for stories, or kids' books, or something?"

"I've done illustrations for stories. Kids' books don't pay my kind of commissions." Her voice was sharp. "Are you criticizing me?"

"No, honey, you're criticizing yourself. I wonder where Charley Retzer is staying?"

"Max would know. Why do you want to see Charley Retzer?"

"Because Charley was out watching the box office on two Giani fights, the two fights right after Giani fought Charley."

"I don't follow you, Luke."

"I was thinking Charley jobbed the Giani fight. And got a piece of Patsy's next two matches in return. If Giani is afraid of an overhand right, I want to know it. That's Charley's best punch."

"But didn't Giani almost kill Charley?"

"Yes. And that's easier when the other man isn't trying."

"You mean Giani would do that, even if he—"

"Even if he knew he was going to win. In some ways, beloved, Patsy's worse than I am." We were driving now, and there was a drugstore about a block ahead. I said, "Stop near that drugstore; I'll call a couple of the boys who should know where Charley's staying."

The boys weren't home, but I got his address from the hospital, the place I should have tried first.

It was a motel on Pico, and there was a light in Charley's unit. There was a sound of a radio, too, and as we came closer the sound of feminine voices, high and shrill.

I knocked, and the voices stopped and Charley's voice said, "That's probably the manager. You babes giggle too much."

"Maybe I'd better wait in the car," Sally said.

"It can't be any worse than the place we ate," I told her.

· Then Charley was in the doorway, framed by the light behind him.

A second, while his eyes focused to the dimness and then: "Champ! Hey, I been trying to get a hold of you."

"Meet my girl, Charley," I said. "You've met Sal before, haven't you?"

"Hell, yes. I'm glad I didn't get a hold of you, Champ. Hi, Sally. Nothing personal, kid."

"How personal can you get?" Sally asked. "I know there are two women in there. Is there, by chance, another man?"

"He's on the way," Charley said easily. "Come on in and meet the folks."

The "folks" looked like a sister act, both synthetic blondes past their prime, one named Vera and one Vickie. Both had fine legs and the kind of brassières that made them look adequately endowed, even if they weren't. These two probably were.

The unit consisted of a living-room and kitchenette and

alcove bedroom. Furnished in rattan, thick with smoke and the girls' perfume.

Charley snapped off the radio. "Drink, Luke?"

"Not unless you have beer. Charley, I've been thinking of fighting Patsy Giani."

"So you told me." The girls had gone to the bathroom, and this room was suddenly very quiet. Sally went over to sit on the rattan davenport.

I said, "You should have licked him, Charley."

"Maybe. I haven't any beer. How about you, Sal?"

From the bathroom came the suppressed giggles of the blondes.

"What are they doing, tickling each other?" Sally asked.

"Ahh," Charley said, "they're good kids. What'll it be, Sal?"

"Nothing," Sally said coolly. And added, "Thank you."

Charley smiled at me. "Why don't you two get married?"

I didn't answer that. "You had a piece of Giani's next two fights after your go with him, didn't you?"

"Not officially." He studied me. "What gives, Luke?"

"I was thinking Giani might have been afraid of you. I mean, his manager; I don't think Patsy's afraid of anybody."

"Neither am I, Luke. That's rough talk. You saying I jobbed it?"

"If you say you didn't, I'll believe you."

"What are you getting at?"

"This—if he was afraid of you, he was afraid of that overhand right, and though a weakness that basic doesn't make sense, better men have had bigger blind spots. I know you got to me with it, in the seventh. If it's true, I'd like you to work out with me for the fight."

"A spar-mate? Me? I should work out with *you*, for that kind of money?"

"For good money. I'd make it worth your while, Charley. And the big gloves and headguards; who'd get hurt?"

Giggling from the bathroom. A sigh from Sally.

Charley shook his head. "You're punchy. I'd like to see Giani get beat; that I'll admit. Would you fight him here?"

"Yes. He didn't have to batter you like he did. Am I right?"

"Maybe. You didn't have to go crazy, either."

"I wasn't quite right, after that punch in the seventh, Charley. Maybe I was rough. I don't remember it."

He looked at me for seconds. "I don't like the guy. I'd hate to see him hold the title. Give me a little time on it, Luke."

"Sure. I'll let you know. Nothing's definite, anyway. Well, keep your tail up, Charley."

"Mmmm-hmmm!" He smiled at Sally. "We're friends?"

She shook her head. "If you want, Luke, I can go home alone. I wouldn't want you to disappoint Vicki. Or was Vera meant for you?"

"They're both for me," Charley said. "I'm a two-gun man. Sally, you don't know when you're well off. You've got the cream of the crop, lady. Treat him right."

Sally said nothing, not even good night.

The giggling started again as we walked to the car and the radio went on.

"Tramp," Sally said.

Nothing from me.

"First Michael with his underwear talk, and now this. Why don't we know some *decent* people?"

"We know us."

"The least he could have done is call it 'lingerie.' And Charley didn't have to give me a sermon. They all think *they're* right, don't they?" She handed me the keys. "You drive for a change."

The Ford coughed into life. Sally sat on the far edge of

the seat from me. She was lighting a cigarette.

I headed the Ford west, toward the ocean.

"Why are all fighters such—beasts? Is it because they were that to begin with? Or is it the fighting that does it?"

"I don't think they're beasts," I said. "Fighting kills some of the—oh, finer instincts in a man, maybe, but—"

"Some? All," Sally said. "The canvas coffin. I wonder how many talents have been buried in a ring?"

"I don't know. Mickey Walker's getting to be quite a painter. But I don't know if he's a good painter, or just a good painter for a former fighter, if you follow me."

"He's good," Sally said. "I've seen his work."

"Well, there's an answer for you. He held three titles and was robbed of the fourth. He'd fight anything up to a platoon. And he's still got his marbles."

"And how about you, Luke Pilgrim?"

"I was always kind of a bastard, I guess. You're not exactly the sweetest girl in the world, yourself, Mrs. Forester."

I cut over to Olympic, and down that, through the tunnel to the Ocean Highway. Sally turned her window down and threw out her cigarette.

The moon was just a sliver in the clear sky, the water barely visible to our left. I cut the flivver into overdrive and snapped on the radio.

In the right-hand lane, just loafing, the Santa Monica bluffs towering to our right, the lights of traffic stretching along the big curve toward Malibu.

"Some day this has been," I said.

No answer from Sally. The radio was giving us the Basin Street Six and the flivver was murmuring to herself.

"This is where I'd like to live," I said. "Near the water."

No comment from my love.

"Up there in the hills," I went on, "a modern house, with a nice sun deck. I could lay there all day and—"

"*Lie* there," Sally corrected me. "Would you be alone?"

"On the sun deck, I'd be alone. You'd be in the house, sweeping and dusting and like that."

"You wouldn't need me. Charley could bring over a couple of floozies."

"Oh, lay off, or lie off, or what the hell it is. Jesus, did I suggest any floozies? Have I ever fiddled with floozies since we met?"

"I don't know. How would I know?"

"If you don't believe in me," I said, "leave me. Don't needle me, just walk out. I wanted to get married. You're the one who doesn't want to get married."

Silence, and then I could hear her slide over, and then a hand was on my knee, squeezing. "I'm sorry, honey. First, that ridiculous bed this morning, and then that nasty Michael Lord and then those peroxide pukes Charley had waiting for you. It's been an awfully depressing day."

"I probably didn't use the bed," I pointed out, "and you didn't marry Michael Lord and even if you hadn't come to town I'd have had nothing to do with Vera or Vickie. You're just a natural sour puss."

"Well, then, what about the underwear crack? You know why that hurts, don't you? Because it's true."

"Well, quit it, then. Go back to serious painting."

"And starve to death? No, thanks." Then she squeezed my knee again. "Look, Luke—seals!"

On the opposite side of the road, here, a seafood place. And next to it, well floodlighted, a huge concrete tank. Three seals were silhouetted against the lights, their necks arched, their heads back, as though baying at the moon.

The road was clear; I swung in a U-turn and pulled into the parking-lot flanking the tank.

As I got out of the car, I was facing the road, and I saw this sedan going by in the direction I'd been traveling. It was only through a lucky combination of light and reflection that the face of the driver was momentarily clear.

It was the big redheaded cop, Sergeant Nolan.

There were one male and two females, barking their hoarse barks, stretching their necks toward us.

"We can get fish at the store here," Sally said. "Let's feed them."

"We're being followed," I said. "Sergeant Nolan just went by."

"Who cares? I'll get the fish."

The three seals stared at me, making not a sound. Then the male arched his neck toward one of the females and groaned some message. She answered, and I got the feeling they were talking about me. And not favorably. They continued to stare.

Sally brought the fish, and we put the seals to work. They flopped and flipped and stretched their smooth necks as they waddled along the board runways. They dove for those we threw in the water, and made general asses of themselves.

"I feel better now," I said. "When they were laughing at me, I felt kind of inferior, but look how silly they get over a few fish."

"Look how silly we all get over a few fish," she said. "Money, money, money— We even do underwear advertisements."

"Honey," I said soothingly, "it sells underwear, as you told Michael. And that puts a lot of people to work. You're contributing to the welfare of all the people who make underwear. Besides, you're not gifted, as you admitted."

We were back in the car now, and she was wiping her hands on a piece of Kleenex. "Don't be so patronizing. Just because you're the champion in your trade, and you know it, don't be so damned lofty and logical."

"I don't know if I'm champ, or not," I said. "That's

why I'm going to fight Giani."

"I thought *that* was why. All the other reasons were a lot of rationalizing. You like the top of your little ant heap, don't you?"

"Mmmm-hmm. And so would you, and just about everybody else. We built a whole civilization on it."

"Please," she said. "You sound like the NAM. I like you better when you talk about things you understand."

"To hell with you," I said.

I jabbed the starter button, goosed the flivver in reverse, scattering gravel.

She was chuckling. "The road-show Walter Lippmann."

I burned quietly, making the flivver hum. The radio had gone on with the ignition; Dixieland blared at us.

Traffic was thin and the Ford logging. Sally reached over to soften the blare of the Dixieland. "I'm sorry, Luke. I'm honestly sorry. But you sounded so—pompous. And I feel so—so unworthy, since dinner."

Ahead a traffic light turned red and I slowed the car.

"That's where Sunset ends," Sally said. "Let's take Sunset back. I like the way it winds."

I cut over to the left lane, saying nothing.

"Don't sulk," Sally said. "What time is it?"

"Nine-thirty."

"We could still see a movie. There's a good one at the Bay. I noticed it this morning."

This morning seemed like a hundred years away. To our right, as we climbed Sunset, was a cult of some sort, and for a moment, I thought I saw a windmill in the moving flash of the headlights.

Then there was a break in the foliage around the pond, and the lights of a car coming down the hill revealed the windmill at the edge of the water.

Sally saw it, too. "Luke, look—"

"I saw it."

"Anything?"

"Nothing."

Her hand was back on my knee. "Friends?"

"I guess."

The old Bernheimer Gardens to our right, the new houses to our right and left, not cheap, but looking raw and temporary. Lights dotting the hills to our left, more new houses, with a view of the sea to the front and the hills all around them.

"Lord, this town has grown," Sally said. "George used to go deer-hunting in those hills, up there."

"Who cares about George?"

"Sears Roebuck. There's the place, Luke."

Redwood and pastel-yellow stucco, the four-unit building that had housed Mary Kostanic, known as Brenda Vane.

Sally imitated the landlady's Midwestern nasal. "Nothing cheap about Brenda." And in her own voice, "Maroon silk sheets. Well, they probably don't show spots."

"I had some maroon silk trunks once. They showed spots."

Nothing from her. A grade and a curve and then climbing, and outlined against the supermarket, the blue neon windmill revolving.

I wondered if we'd lost the sergeant, or if he had been traveling the road on some other business. It didn't seem possible he could have been tailing us all day. He couldn't have; he'd been at the station when I'd phoned this afternoon.

"Here's the show," Sally said. "There's a parking-lot on the other side of it."

It was a sentimental picture, and we held hands. We came out after twelve, and took Sunset all the way back to the hotel. I was bushed, emotionally and physically spent by the day behind us.

As we walked into the hotel, she said, "We haven't learned anything, have we? Chasing around like a couple of nitwits—"

"We learned some things at *Harry's Hoot Owl Club.* Not much after that."

She got her key from the desk. Max was already in the room, so our key was up there.

She was on our floor; we went up together in the elevator. I wondered if there was a way I could ask Sergeant Sands about the light in Brenda's apartment.

If the light was off, when she was discovered, someone had been there after I had. The killer. Though turning out a light wouldn't be proof of murder. And there wasn't any way I could think of to ask Sands without implicating myself.

We were walking along the hall now, and we came to Sally's door. I stopped and looked at her inquiringly.

She put a hand on her lips, and then on mine. "Don't brag, Champ; you're as tired as I am. Pretend you've started your training."

Her smile was weary. The door closed behind her.

Chapter VIII

IN THE DREAM they were sewing this body in canvas. It was the deck of a ship, but you couldn't see the water. There was a big seam right up the middle of the canvas, and now only the face was still uncovered.

Harry Bevilaqua stood next to me on the deck of the ship. He was telling the men how to sew. Then he turned to me. "You want to get a last look at the face, Champ? We're about ready to dump him."

I came closer and bent to see the face in the dim moonlight.

It was my own.

I opened my eyes and saw the shadows in the room. The bed beneath me was damp, and my pajamas were wet. Max snored in a ragged rhythm.

My mind went back over the Giani fights I'd seen, the brawling, bloody, anything-goes battles he'd fought, trying to get to me. A buller and a hitter, a flat-footed slugger, knocking over anything that stood in his way, the shadow of the mob over him like the broad top of a tornado.

Young. And ready. Never out of shape. Carrying a grudge for Luke Pilgrim, a cheese champ in his mind. Cherishing the crown, scorning the man who held it.

Noodles wanted to be ringside when Patsy beat my brains out. Who else would sit with Noodles, waiting for the ax? All the half-wise guys, the gents who got a word here and there and fashioned it into a belief that prevented their full knowing.

But that wouldn't include Max. And how about the sports writers? In most towns, the sports writers know only a little more than the true fans. In Los Angeles, they knew considerably less. In Los Angeles, the publicity town, even the sports writers believed their own ridiculous publicity. Unless they weren't leveling in their columns. Which could be.

It's a name-conscious town, and I was the champion of the world. The fight would get ink; the fight would draw, and pay. Even wrestling was profitable in this sports-hungry town. Even wrestling got ink, though there was a story about that.

So, win or lose, it would be big money. Isn't that what I wanted?

No, I wanted to see him go down. I wanted to hit him, and see him fold. I wanted to kill him.

Max stopped in mid-snore, gurgled, and turned over. "The bastards," Max mumbled. "Dirty bastards." His breathing was heavy and uneven.

"Hit 'im again, Max, he's Irish," I said.

He started to snore.

I stretched and turned, trying to relax. The memory of the dream came to me, and I forced it from my mind. As a kid, going to church, the thought of death hadn't brought the shivers. Sally had said only cowards believed in God. Sally said if we hadn't had a God, we'd have invented one. But Sally said a lot of damn-fool things.

A muscle twitched in my thigh; it felt like something crawling on me, and I jerked. I was wide awake and nervous. My God, I was actually scared.

I went into the main room and turned on a light and picked up the paper Max had evidently bought tonight. It was tomorrow morning's *Times* and there was a piece about the possibility of my fighting Giani. The writer thought it could easily be the battle of the century.

I stretched out on the davenport with the rest of the paper. And fell asleep.

It was Max's voice that wakened me, arguing on the phone. "Nothing's definite, yet. What the hell kind of statement can I give you when nothing's definite? Sure, sure, when it is, I will. That's what we live on, publicity."

He turned from the phone to look at me. "How long you been there? You know you can catch cold, sleeping like that? You ain't got a damned bit of sense."

"Relax," I told him. "You're like a crazy man lately."

"Somebody's got to worry," he said. He sat down in one of the twin chairs and stared across the room at me. "You act like nobody's died."

"You're not implicated in that, Max. You're clear."

His face hardened. He said nothing.

"You used to be so cheerful, Max. And why do you quibble with Sally all the time? Sally's a good kid."

He said, "You're determined to fight that son-of-a-bitch, aren't you? You've got some idea you can lick him."

"I want to know. But I won't try it without you, Max. I wouldn't fight anybody without you in the corner."

He looked away from me, looking at nothing, his eyes sad. He looked back. "They'd like to make it as soon as possible. That sport bowl's about done, and they'd like to get the title as quick as they can."

"That's all right. Every day I get older. See if you can find a training-spot near Malibu, huh? We'll give it the big treatment, charge for workouts. They love that crap out here. We'll milk it, Max. Smile, huh? You don't look right without a smile."

"Why Malibu?"

"There's some seals I like to watch out there. No, I want to be near the water. Smile, Max?"

Sort of half-smile, but better than nothing.

"Phone Sally. We'll all eat together here. Go ahead, call her."

"Boy, you're sure charged up this morning." He went to the phone, shaking his head, as I went for a shower and shave.

Hit 'em, hit 'em, hit 'em—how I love to hit 'em. And Patsy is a boy who can be hit. Maybe not hurt, but he could be hit. The shower dug at me and the room filled with steam and I felt about eighteen years old.

I was dressed when Sally came. She kissed Max on the nose and he patted her rump, and we all sat down, friends again.

Max said, "We can make 'em bleed. We can get a piece of his next two fights; we can hog the gate. They're hungry for that title."

"And a rematch if I lose."

He smiled at me. "If?"

"If."

"Sure, that, too. D'Amico's coming over this morning. With Patsy."

"And Krueger?"

"I don't know about Dutch. There's a rumor he's out. D'Amico'll probably put some stooge in as a noodle. They probably figure you're going to dive."

"Let 'em."

Max shook his head. "No. That I want stated, by you, before we sign anything."

"Okay. Isn't Sally pretty this morning?"

"Sally's always pretty," Max said. "God knows why she sticks to a bullhead like you."

"I'm not sticking to either of you this morning," she said. "I had too much masculine company yesterday. To-day I shop alone."

"Any time you go shopping, it will be alone," I agreed.

"Even after we're married."

She kissed us both, before she left. And asked me, why didn't I fill in the time until D'Amico came with a little reading?

There wasn't that much time. He came about fifteen minutes after Sally left. Four of them came, crowding the room, D'Amico, Wald, Patsy. And Johnny.

Patsy shook my hand like a brother Elk, and said genially, "It's about time, eh, Champ?"

"About," I said. "Where's Dutch?"

Patsy's big shoulders shrugged, and his flat, attractive face grimaced skeptically. "I don't know about the politics, Champ. Wald's my new noodle."

I laughed. I couldn't help it. Wald.

Wald's tanned face flushed a bit. "I don't intend to be a handler, too. We can hire all the boys we want for that."

"Not like Dutch, you can't," Max said. "But that's your business."

Johnny stood near the door, staring at nothing, as usual.

D'Amico said, "Well, let's get the axes out."

"One thing, first," I said. "Yesterday, I may have given you boys a bad steer. I've got to have Max in the corner, and any time Max is there, it's on the up and up. No other deal."

I looked at D'Amico as I said this, letting him read whatever he wanted to read in my blank face. He was smiling when I'd finished.

Patsy said, "Hell, Champ, all of us want it straight. That's the way it's always been with me."

Clean, flat face, young eyes, and he could lie without a quiver. What a phony. Until he pulled the gloves on.

D'Amico chuckled. Johnny looked his way. Wald frowned, and I could guess he was trying to figure me.

"Before we start," Max said, "this you guys know. I could keep you from that title the rest of your lives. You all understand that?"

Wald frowned, and started to say something. But D'Amico said, "I guess you're right, Max. *You're*—clean enough. You're solid, all right."

But Max didn't do the fighting. And *me*, they thought they had over a barrel.

The chiseling started. I was as silent as Johnny, which put Max up against the three of them. Or two and a half of them; Patsy didn't offer much. All Patsy really wanted was me in a ring. At any price.

Max came out on top, as usual. Max threw names around like Winchell, filling the room with prominence.

When they'd left, he went around opening windows. The deal was all oral, so far, and they'd probably try to chisel when it came to typing it up, but Max and our lawyer would be ready for that, too.

He opened the last of the windows, and turned to face me. "I never thought I'd see this day," he said.

"You'd better phone the newspapers."

"Wald's handling that. *That*, he knows."

I laughed. "Sam Wald, manager. Golly. I wonder if he's ever *seen* a fight?"

"I wonder what's happened to Dutch. Maybe we could get to him, think?"

"I don't know. You know as much about Giani as Dutch does. You never missed one of his fights, did you?"

"None I could help. That's why I ducked him, among other reasons."

"All I can do is lose. He isn't going to kill me."

"You hope. I'm going to take a hot bath. I'm jumpy." He started to peel off his shirt. "That Johnny—"

I took off my shirt, too, and went out to the patio for some more sun. There was no sun; it was clouding up and too cool to enjoy.

I came in and stretched out on the davenport. I was

sleepy, now that everything was settled. Against the monotone of the water running in the tub, I dozed. Later I heard Max on the phone, and still later the beat of the rain on the windows.

It was a corker. The water was curb-high in less than an hour. In two hours, Sepulveda was closed by a slide and there'd been a two-lane slide on the Pacific Coast Highway.

"We'd better forget about getting to Malibu today," Max complained.

"Today?" I asked. "You are in a hurry, aren't you? Hell, Max, I've been fighting, right along. I'm in shape."

"Not for Giani. You still off gin rummy?"

"No. I'll play."

He shuffled the cards slowly. "I keep thinking of that girl, that poor tramp. You don't think those bastards staged this whole thing, do you?"

"Killed a girl to get a fight with me? No. Hell, no."

I went down in four draws and caught Max with over fifty in his hand. It set the pattern for the rest of it; I butchered him. The rain was lighter, but still steady.

Max must have been thinking of the girl all the time. Because when we went down to lunch, he said, "Well, if they didn't kill her, who the hell did?"

"I seem to be the only logical choice, so far."

"Nuts," Max said. "The law wouldn't get off your neck if they thought you were mixed up in it at all."

As we went through the lobby to the grille, I saw the big man with the red hair sitting where he had a view of the desk. Sergeant Nolan, earning his money.

The rain continued. Van Nuys was flooded. Lincoln Boulevard was under water. There'd been a slide in Topanga Canyon.

"Still love this country, Max?" I asked.

"I'm not getting wet," he said. "That cab driver said

the light was on when you left this girl's apartment, huh?"

"That's right. I was trying to think of a way to ask Sergeant Sands if the light was on when her body was discovered."

"How could you ask that? You couldn't."

"That's what I've decided."

Up in the suite again, Max phoned and I napped. The windmills came back at me, a pair of them, this time, and Harry Bevilaqua's mammoth face was mixed up in it somehow.

I was only half asleep and the rise and fall of Max's voice as he phoned was in the background with the drip of the rain.

I'd waited outside for Noodles. Had Brenda put me out? Or was I waiting with blood on my hands? I remembered Sergeant Sands's examination of my hands. What had that meant? Was some of the killer's flesh back there when they found her? If you break any teeth with an early blow, that could happen. A broken tooth will gouge out a chunk of hand.

The stuffed owl looked at me from the back of Harry's bar. There was something there in Harry's bar, all right. I remembered how relieved Noodles had been when he'd learned of my blackout.

"Okay, Joe," Max was saying. "That's damned white of you. We'll take good care of the place. Sounds like just the spot we want."

He hung up the phone and snapped on the radio. I rolled over and sat up. "What's new?"

"Got a spot, I think. In Malibu. You know, this brawl could put you on Queer Street, but good. You know that, don't you? After that blackout you had, and all."

"I suppose. Who's this Joe?"

"One of my rich friends. He's even got a scaffolding for a ring out there. Tommy Burke used to train out there when they were trying to build him into a local draw."

"Tommy Burke," I said, and yawned. "He's selling roofing in Milwaukee now."

"So? So what?"

"Nothing. Just making conversation. I wonder where Sally is?"

"Probably nosing into the murder. She didn't fool me with that shopping gag."

"Are you a Russian Jew or a German Jew, Max?" I asked.

"Bronx Jew. Why? You anti-Semitic, or something?"

"No, I was thinking some days you're as hard to get along with as the Russians. Why shouldn't Sally be shopping?"

"We'll see what she buys," he said. "I'll give you even money she doesn't come home with a thing."

"Fifty," I said. "Even money. You've got a bet."

It wasn't twenty seconds after that there was a knock on the door, and then it opened and Sally came in, her arms full of packages.

I started to laugh, and she said, "I've had a talk with Ruth, Luke. She's Noodles's girl friend. Imagine that!"

"No bet," Max said. "We were both right."

Sally looked between us. "What's all this?"

"A bet. Who's Ruth?"

"The girl at the end of the bar, the one reading the *Racing Form*. The one Harry made powder her nose, remember? She knows all about horses, Luke. She's gone with a lot of jockeys. She likes small men, she told me. But Noodles, Gawd!"

"Sit down and calm down," I said. "Did you go to Harry's place *alone?*"

She stacked her packages on one of the chairs and sat in another. She took a lot of time finding a cigarette and lighting it, before she looked at me. Then she nodded humbly.

"And Harry let you talk to that girl?"

"He wasn't there."

"What kind of—" I shook my head. "You're crazy."

"Maybe. She gave me a couple of horses. I wrote them down. Cinches, she said."

"Mudders, I hope," Max said.

Sally nodded, looking at Max. "Mudders." She looked back at me. "We talked for almost half an hour, in one of the booths. She said something's bothering Noodles; he's been very cranky the last couple of days. She lives with Noodles, but they're not married. Like us, sort of."

"What else did she tell you?"

"That's about it. She says Noodles doesn't confide in her much. She said she'd tell me almost anything. She likes me."

"I'll bet. Maybe she was playing you for a patsy. Did that thought occur to you?"

"Don't be stuffy, pug. Do you want to see what I bought?"

"I can't wait," I said.

Sweaters, she'd bought, cashmere, three of them. A simple little black suit. An angora scarf. "And," she finished with, "a present for Max. Because we're friends."

She threw him five wax-paper-covered wads.

Bubble gum.

Max smiled, and looked at her thoughtfully. "Training starts tomorrow. We've got a place in Malibu. *Strict* training starts tomorrow."

"Don't be cryptic, Max. Say what you mean clearly."

"I mean, starting tomorrow you two feel sentimental, you can hold hands."

"You're being vulgar, Max." She winked at me.

"I'm wording it as clean as I can. Something's got to be said. I want Luke in the best shape he's known in years.

Not because I figure he's got any chance to win, but because the better his shape, the less permanent damage Giani is likely to do. No part of this brawl was my idea, you'll remember. But I'm going along with it, so it's going to be my way. You love the guy, that's the way you'll want it, too."

"I love the guy, Max. *Tomorrow* it starts?"

"Tomorrow."

"Baby," Sally said to me, "what are you doing tonight?"

Above the city, this place was, the lights below us. The air was clean, after the rain, clean and cold. The bed was one of those king-sized beds Sally had called ridiculous.

"I was wrong about that," she said. "Luke, we're like animals."

"Right."

"It's not all we have though, is it?"

"I never think of it that way. You do, all the time. Maybe it's all we have to you."

"No, no, no—Luke, you're—strange. Sometimes you don't seem to be in this world. I can't reach you at all."

"Own me, you mean, not reach me. Nobody owns me."

"Could you live without me?"

"Sure. But not well. You could live without me, too."

Dimness, relaxed, at peace, asleep. No dreams, a void. Waking to darkness and the shadowed silhouette of Sally against the lights. She sat near the bank of windows on the buttressed side, smoking.

"Come and see the lights, Luke."

She had a cigarette waiting for me. Lights in rows, the streets leading out across the valley floor. Jutting out of the side of a mountain, this place. Belonging to a friend.

"That bed," Sally said. "I see Brenda's point."

"Shut up about Brenda."

"Why?"

"Because we're here, and alive. Nobody can help Brenda any more."

"Or hurt her," Sally said quietly.

She was looking out at the lights. "I wonder how many are sleeping? Do you think Noodles and Ruth are sleeping?"

"I don't know. You're not going back to Chicago, just because I'm going to be training, are you?"

"Not if you want me here."

"I want you here. Are you sleepy? Do you want to go back to bed?"

"I'm not sleepy. Let's go back to bed."

Back at the hotel, Max said, "That Coast Highway is open again. We can go out and look at the place in Malibu this morning."

"I'm going along," Sally said. "I can rent a cottage."

Max frowned.

Sally said, "Holding hands only. That's a promise, Max."

"All right, all right. You still disturb him, don't you?"

"She'd disturb me if she was in Chicago, too," I told him.

"All right, all right, *all right!*"

About a hundred yards from the water, this home was. Glass brick and natural stone, one story high and spread all over the landscape, an immense place.

The training ring was under the protecting branches of a eucalyptus tree.

"What a silly place for it," Sally said. "Those seed pods will be dropping in the ring all the time."

"My national tree," Max said. "We can put netting over the ring."

The canvas of the ring was frayed and rotted; the padding was useless. But that could be repaired.

The house had five bedrooms and five baths, a living-room no more than fifty feet long with a high hearth fire-place just large enough to accommodate a roasting ox.

"My kind of living," Sally said. "Where's the owner, Max?"

"In Las Vegas. He runs a club there. Sally, you might as well stay here, too. You could handle some of the publicity and the paper work, and all."

"And you could keep an eye on Luke and me."

Max sighed, looking aggrieved. "Suit yourself."

"I'll stay." She plopped down in one of the room's nine-foot davenports. "What a vulgar display of wealth." She looked at me. "This, you could have, if you'd saved your money."

"Let's get our stuff," Max said. "Let's get the ball rolling. You two can handle the hauling, can't you?"

Max stayed out there, to wait for the telephone men and the other utility connections. Sally and I went back to the hotel.

There was a message for me at the desk. There were three of them, actually, but all from the same person. They'd been phoned in.

"Some man named Noodles," the clerk said. "And you can reach him at that address there. He doesn't want you to phone."

The address was in the poor district of Santa Monica, in the colored district off Olympic. Sally drove; she can make a lot better time than I can.

A small, leaning frame house, the front yard fenced with chicken wire, the gray lawn beyond recall. Next door a dog was howling, as we came up the path through the yard to the rotted front porch.

"That dog," Sally said. "I'm—"

I knocked on the thin front door, and there was no sound.

I knocked again, and heard a low moan from inside. It was a woman's voice.

"Open the door," Sally said. "There's something wrong here; I *know* it, Luke. That howling dog—"

The door was open, and I went through it ahead of Sally.

A faded rug, a battered velour davenport, a chair to match. A television set and a contour chair, looking out of place in that sad room.

The moaning came from a doorway to the right. A small hall leading to the bathroom and the bedroom. The moaning was coming from the bedroom.

Linoleum on the floor in here, a painted iron bedstead, a cigarette-scarred bird's-eye maple chiffonier, a straight chair, and an oilcloth-covered chest. The window was open; the slight breeze stirred the grimy curtain.

In the corner of the room, sitting on the floor, holding her hands tightly in her lap and rocking from side to side, the girl from the bar, the girl named Ruth.

Moaning quietly, rocking methodically, staring out at nothing, she was in shock.

On top of the unmade bed, a quiet small body, one small hand clenching a handful of his own shirt, the other hand and arm extending stiffly down his side, the man known as Noodles.

Noodles, too, was staring, but he wasn't in shock.

Noodles was dead.

Chapter IX

BEHIND ME, a choked murmur came from Sally's throat. I turned to see her paper-white face, to see her waver on her feet.

"Steady, baby," I said, and came to put an arm around her. "We'd better phone the police. If there isn't a phone here, we'll have to go next door."

Footsteps in the living-room, coming our way, and I called, "Who's there?"

No answer, but a moment later he stood in the doorway from the hall. The redheaded cop, Sergeant Nolan.

He came into the room, stared from Ruth to Noodles, and then at us.

"He's been phoning me all morning," I said. "He probably had something to tell me."

"Get to a phone," he said wearily. "Get Sergeant Sands here, and an ambulance. And then call the local police. We can't sit on this one any more. *This* is Santa Monica."

The captain said, "We want to co-operate, Sergeant, of course. We always have. But let's not rush things."

In a small bright room, the four of us. Sergeant Sands and Sally and I and Captain Aaronsen of the Santa Monica police.

Big, blond man, the captain, dwarfing the desk in front of him, smiling out at the three of us, one of those calm

Swedes.

"There's no doubt in my mind," Sands said, "that this is directly connected with the death of Brenda Vane. I can guarantee you that Pilgrim is clean on this kill. Sergeant Nolan went with him to that house."

"*After* him," Aaronsen corrected him gently.

"With him, in a department car. They took two cars, but they went together. I'd like to have you release this Ruth Gonzales to my custody, too, when you're finished with her."

"We'll get along, Sergeant. Let's be patient. Those statements should be ready in a few minutes." He smiled at all of us.

From there to the west-side station. From there, Sands drove us back to our car, still in front of the little house.

We hadn't learned anything, Sally and I. Whether Noodles had been stabbed, shot, or poisoned we didn't know. What Ruth Gonzales had told the police, we didn't know.

As he pulled up behind our car, Sands said, "You'll be fighting Giani, I hear."

"That's right."

"I hope you kill him." His voice rough with emotion.

"Oh? You think Giani's behind this murder, Sergeant?"

"D'Amico. And he's behind Giani. And they pressured you into the fight, didn't they?"

"They think they did. I wanted them to think they did. I need all the weapons I can find for that battle, Sergeant."

He studied me. "I could be wrong about you, but I've been working on the theory that you're clean, and a credit to the game. Giani isn't. Wald isn't. D'Amico sure as hell isn't. But you're not working with me."

"I've been trying to save my neck," I said. I took a deep breath. "I—"

"Luke, shut up," Sally said.

"No," I said. "Sergeant, I may have killed Brenda Vane. I don't remember any of the things that happened from the seventh round of the fight until the next morning."

"So? How about your manager?"

"He tried to protect me. Brenda dropped him off at the hotel first and she and I went on from there. Probably to her apartment. Noodles picked me up in front of her apartment, he told me, and took me back to the hotel. He doesn't know, *didn't* know if Brenda was alive then or not. There was a light on in her apartment, but he didn't see her."

"That's what he told you, that day in the *Hoot Owl Club?*"

"That's right. I think he was lying; I had a feeling he was trying to protect somebody. Otherwise, why didn't he go to the police with what he knew about it?"

"That would be too simple," Sands said bitterly. "That way, he'd be alive, today."

"What killed him?" I asked.

"Conine. Rye whisky, loaded with conine. His own bottle, right there in the house. You figure that one. Who but the girl? But who paid her to do it?"

"Ruth wouldn't," Sally said. "I know she wouldn't. She really loved him, Sergeant."

"Love—" the sergeant said. "The smart thing to do would be to put you and your manager away, Pilgrim. And then build up a case. A good prosecutor could probably get a conviction just on what you've told me."

I said nothing. Sally started to cry, and I put an arm around her.

"Only the hell of it is," the sergeant went on, "you're not the killer, and I'm the simple kind of bastard who lets a little thing like that bother him."

Sally stopped crying. A great peace moved through me.

"How do you know I'm innocent?" I heard my own

voice ask. "Because of the hands, Sergeant?"

"That's part of it. And I could be wrong, too. D'Amico and his boys must know you went home with Brenda. How do they know it?"

"They don't, probably. They played a hunch, because Wald knows I left with the girl. I don't know how they learned about Noodles. That's *their* kill—Noodles?"

"Who knows? That Bevilaqua knows more than he told us. But you could work him over with an ax and get no more than he wants to tell you." He shook his head. "Isn't there *anything* you remember about that night?"

"The windmill. That bakery trade-mark on the front of the supermarket on Sunset, there in the Palisades. I keep dreaming about the thing, about *two* of them, lately. But it doesn't make any sense to me."

"All right. You're still at the hotel?"

"No. We'll be moving out to Malibu, to go into training. I don't know the address, but I'll phone it in to you."

"That place where Burke trained?"

"That's it."

"I know the place. I'll be seeing you, out there. Don't keep anything else from me, Pilgrim."

"I won't."

"And work. Be ready for that guy, be right."

"I mean to, Sergeant. Still betting?"

"Beat it," he said. "I'll be seeing you."

We got out of the department car, and Sally said, "You drive, Luke." She was crying again. "That poor little man. Why, Luke, why did he have to die?"

"So they could keep the heat on, they think. Or maybe the killer. I don't know. Don't think about it, Sal."

"He likes you, that Sergeant Sands. He's certainly going along with you." She blew her nose. "He must believe in you."

"Maybe. Maybe he's giving me enough rope to hang

myself with, too." I put a hand over hers. "Don't tell Max I spouted to the law. He's fretting enough now."

"I won't. Luke, I just thought of something. I'll bet I know why he admitted he thought you were innocent. Because he didn't want you to worry, before this fight. He wanted you to be ready for this fight. It's D'Amico he really hates. Anything else is secondary with him."

"That could be. There's some sense to that. There's no other reason I can think of why he'd let me know I wasn't his number-one suspect."

"That girl, the way she stared. She must have loved him. She couldn't have poisoned him, not Ruth, could she?"

"Don't think about it."

"How can I stop?"

"Think about the moving. Think about the fight, anything but this morning."

"Morning?" she said. "Migosh, Max is out there without transportation. I'll bet he's starving. What time is it?"

It was almost two. It was after three when we started for Malibu with the luggage.

Max wasn't at the house. Max was at the roadside restaurant, picking his teeth and watching the seals. We almost missed him breezing as we were.

I swung the flivver in a U-turn and came back.

"No hurry," he said acidly. "Did you have some shopping to do?"

"Noodles has been killed," I said. "Poisoned."

"Noodles? Who the hell's Noodles?"

"That cab driver, the one who brought me home from the girl's apartment."

Max was in the act of getting into the car, and he paused, to stare at me. Seconds passed, and he said, "D'Amico. This time I'd make book on it."

We made the rest of the trip in silence.

We put away our clothes, each to a bedroom, and then a man came with a load of groceries, and I helped Sally stow those away in the kitchen.

Max came in as we were finishing. "There's some more bedrooms and a bath over the garage. The help can stay there. I want to get Tony Scarpa, for one. The rest can come from town."

Tony Scarpa was an overweight welter, a fighter more or less in the Giani pattern, though a hell of a lot smoother.

I said, "I think Charley Retzer will work out with us, too. Charley doesn't like Giani. I've talked to him."

"You boys sure love to spend money," Sally said. "Is all this necessary?"

"It'll pay," Max said. "We're going to have the biggest gate in middleweight history, I'll guarantee you that. And this town goes for a lot of front."

"Maybe," Sally said, "we could get a couple of those searchlights and some bright bunting. This fight's had too much publicity already."

"How do you figure that?" Max asked.

Sally looked at me. I looked at Max, and said, "I—we, Sally and I found Noodles's body, Max. We called the police. Or no, the police followed us; Sergeant Nolan, it was."

Max opened his mouth, and closed it. He opened it again, looking like the papa seal waiting for a fish. He closed it again, turned on his heel, and left the kitchen.

"Max—wordless," Sally said. "I'll bet it's the first time in history."

"Let's eat something," I said. "I'm starving."

It was what is known as a farm kitchen, with its own fireplace and eating-section and lounging-area. Sally made an omelette with cheese and toasted some rye bread and made coffee, and we ate in the dining-section, where we could see the ocean.

No sign of Max, no sounds from him.

"He's sulking," Sally said. "Let's have our coffee in the living-room."

That's where Max was. He'd built a fire in the huge fireplace and was sitting on the davenport in front of it, a drink in one hand.

"You might have told us about the fire," Sally said, "so we could all enjoy it." She went over to sit next to him on the davenport. "Don't be unhappy, Max."

I went over to sit on the other side of him.

"I'm scared," he said simply.

"Why?" I asked. "You grew up with mugs. And you've got more influential friends than Jim Farley. You've no reason to be scared."

"I'm old and tired and scared. Neither one of you know enough about D'Amico's kind of people. I'm getting old and I earned some peace. But you two have to play cop."

"We didn't, Max. When we got to the hotel there was a message for me. Noodles had phoned three times and wanted to see me. I went over there, and he was dead. Sergeant Nolan had followed us over."

"So maybe if you hadn't got to him in Bevilaqua's bar that afternoon and maybe if Sally hadn't worked on his girl friend, maybe this Noodles would still be alive. One thing I did learn, growing up with those kind of people, was to mind my own damned business. That way, *everybody's* better off."

"I can't accept that, Max," Sally said. "But let's not fight about it. We've enough to fight without fighting each other." She put a hand on his.

He sighed, staring at the fire. "I never used to be scared, and God knows I had reason to be. Maybe I didn't have so much to live for, then. Or maybe I wanted more than I do now."

The fire highlighted his broad, sad face. He leaned back

and closed his eyes. Sally took the empty glass from his hand.

"Relax, Max," she said.

"Fall asleep, you mean? What about you two? I want to keep an eye on you two."

"You've my solemn promise, Max."

His eyes were still closed as he patted her hand. "I know. You're all right, Sally. We want the best for Luke, don't we? We love that bullheaded bastard, don't we?"

"Most times. I wish he was more like you, though. You've got more sense, Max. And more heart."

"Yeah, but I ain't got his 'built,' like we say in the Bronx. There's a television set if you two get bored. There's four of 'em. Gawd."

"Maybe there's a library, too," Sally said. "Let's see if there's a library, Luke."

There was no library. A den, but no library.

"Four television sets," Sally said, "at five hundred each, we'll say. That's two thousand dollars. For three dollars and ninety-five cents, he can get a complete Shakespeare. But he'd rather spend two thousand dollars to watch Milton Berle. No wonder people like D'Amico can take over."

"The road-show Walter Lippmann," I said. "Please talk about things you understand."

"All right, we're even. Luke, look at that moon."

A full moon, over the quiet water, shining through the full-length windows flanking the fireplace.

"Let's go out," Sally said. "I'll get a coat."

I got one, too, and we went out into the chill California night, and down to the beach. Behind us, the glass brick of the house gleamed in reflection.

"Runs a club in Las Vegas," Sally said. "Why is it the wrong people have all the money?"

"The road-show Walter Lippmann," I said, and she said, "Oh, shut up. I'm sorry I cut off your curbstone philosophy last night but you were being very banal."

"Okay, then. The wrong people have all the money because the right people have the wrong appetites."

"Like—"

"Like gambling and entertainment and adultery and alcohol. So the gamblers and the movie stars and the divorce lawyers and distillers wind up with all the money, naturally."

"And the *smart* fighters," Sally said.

"And the underwear artists with sense."

"*Commercial* artists, counterpuncher."

"Yes. Commercial artists."

We walked along the beach, just out of reach of the water, where the sand was wet and hard. Overhead, a big plane droned, its lights alternately blinking. On the highway, the car lights brightened the hills crowding the road.

"Poor Max," Sally said.

"Poor Luke. Max doesn't have to fight him."

"Poor Noodles."

"And Brenda."

"All right, and Brenda. Luke, could you kiss me without getting all riled up?"

"Of course." I held her lightly by the shoulders and kissed her eyelids. "After I put this Giani out of commission, after I fix him so he'll never want to fight again, you and I are going to get married. Or we are going to call it quits."

"All right. I'm ready for it. Luke, what do you mean about Giani? You were never a spoiler, Luke. Isn't that the word, 'spoiler'?"

"That's the word. And don't talk about my streak. And don't argue about it, and think what you damned please. Giani I mean to fix, good. For reasons of my own and reasons of my trade."

"If you can. Nobody thinks you can."

"Nobody thought Dempsey could take Willard. But he knocked him down seven times in the first round. Don't worry about what people think."

"All right. You're my gospel."

She kissed my neck and the silver of her hair was like a mist in my vision.

"Let's go back," I said. "I want to hit the hay early."

Only one more think did she have to say, and that about halfway back to the house.

"The canvas coffin," she said.

A dreamless night on a good hard bed, and Max shaking me awake at eight o'clock. He had a sweat shirt on and corduroy trousers and tennis shoes.

"C'mon," he said, "that beach is just right for road work."

"Before breakfast?"

"Right. Let's go."

Max looks like a little fat man until you trot along beside him for a while. Then he looks like a little stocky man. I was blowing, and he was still breathing free and easy by the time we got back to the house.

Sally had breakfast ready, and the table set in that big kitchen. I didn't have time to dawdle over it. Max had me out splitting firewood the minute I was through eating.

Tony Scarpa came out around ten-thirty in a weathered station wagon. He parked not far from where I was working and grinned out at me.

"For this one, you'll work. Luke, baby, you went over the edge?"

"Make sense," I said.

"Giani," he explained. "Muggsy Ellis or Art Cary, sure. Or another battle of the century with Charley Retzer. But Giani. Did you get a piece of him, or something?"

"Blow it," I said. "Wait'll I get you in a ring."

He came out of the station wagon. "Oh, me, a lousy

welter, sure."

"You don't look like a welter to me," I said. "What do you go now, Tony?"

He shrugged. "Hundred and fifty, sixty. Depends on how I eat." He held out a hand. "I hope you do it, Champ."

A different tone, that last sentence. I shook his hand. "Good to see you, Tony. Think I'm out of my class?"

"I haven't seen you go for two years," he said. "Four years ago, nobody was good enough for you." He looked past me. "Hey!"

Sally stood there in shorts and one of the new sweaters.

"*My* girl, Tony," I said. "Sally, I'd like to present Tony Scarpa, Sally Forester."

"A distinct pleasure," Tony said. "Your house, Miss Forester?"

She shook her head. "One of Max's many friends. Luke, Charley Retzer phoned. He's coming out, too."

"Fine," I said.

"I told him to leave Vera and Vickie behind, though."

Tony grinned. "I had a date with Vera, couple nights ago. Don't we need a cook?"

Sally looked at him wonderingly. "Two nights ago, or three?"

Tony frowned. "Let's see—three. I fixed Charley up with Vickie, and—"

But Sally wasn't listening. Sally came over to kiss me on the nose. "I misjudged you, honey."

"What goes on?" Tony asked. Over Sally's shoulder, he winked at me, and gave me the nod.

"Nothing you'd understand," Sally said.

Then Max was out there, and Max said, "Hello, Tony. I'll show you where you're bedding down." He looked at the wood I'd split. "We'll need more than that."

Tony went to get his luggage. Sally said, "See you later,

Champ," and went into the house.

I was left with the wood and the ax.

The men came out to repair the ring. Charley Retzer came, a colored handler named Jest came. I stayed with the wood.

Until Max came out to say lunch was ready. "I had a cook coming," he said, "but Sally wants to handle it. Don't ask me why. It'll be a lot of work."

"Work never bothered Sally. It does me, though. My back aches, Max. Maybe I sprained something."

"Sure. Let's go."

Steak for lunch, broiled over charcoal on the big grille in the big kitchen. Salad with garlic dressing and milk, milk, milk.

Tony Scarpa said, "I thought only wops liked garlic."

"Italians," Sally corrected him, and wondered why we laughed.

The big bag, that afternoon, boom-boom-boom. The little bag, tat-a-tat-tat. The rope. And then a couple fast ones with Tony Scarpa. Max had taped my bad hand with Plastora.

He hit me with everything he threw, damned near. He looked fat and out of shape, but Tony could always move. He moved around me, sliding in, sliding out, smooth as only an old-timer can be, scoring, splat, splat, splat.

"Jesus Christ, Luke," he said, when it was over.

"Max has got me muscle-bound," I complained. "He's working me too hard, too early. And that bum right hand slowed me."

"Maybe," he said.

It wasn't true, but I didn't want to bring Sally into it. It would come back. Milk and eggs and steak and the fresh air; it would come back.

Max had some movies for us, after that. Giani's fights with Art Cary, with Graziano, with Charley Retzer.

In the Retzer fight, in the fifth round, there was a fine camera angle on the right hand Charley hit him with. For almost two seconds, Giani was motionless, his hands low, his eyes blank. Charley was flat on his feet, the right cocked, and Charley, too, remained motionless. Then Giani started to retreat, his hands up.

Tony Scarpa's laugh was edged in the dim room. "Could we have that one over? Oh, Charley!"

"Wise guy," Charles said. "Anybody can make a mistake."

"And how," Tony said. "The Commission made the big mistake on that one."

"Wise guy," Charley said again.

"Shut up, you two," Max said.

There wasn't much I learned from the pictures that I didn't already know. Patsy was hit often enough, but only Charley had slowed him. Patsy bulled in, working close to his man, one big shoulder protecting his chin, doing all the legal and illegal damage he could get away with in the clinch.

Three times the camera showed him hitting on the break, a dozen blows looked low. The laces and the elbows and the top of his thick head were additional Giani weapons.

But Charley knew all those tricks and more; Charley had invented a couple new ones. And he'd be working out with me.

When the room grew bright again, Tony said, "You've been fighting right along, Champ. Why all the trappings?"

"Los Angeles," I said. "And a dead sports time for the papers. This fight is going to be milked. Wait'll you see the ticket scale."

Max and Charley and Jest and Tony played pinochle; I took a hot bath, soaking in the big tub, stretching the soreness out, feeling the tenseness leave and my mind quieting down.

Clean slacks and flannel sport shirt, at peace and spot-less. In the car-barn living-room the boys were still at the pinochle, shrouded in the smoke of Max's cigar.

In the kitchen, Sally sat near the fireplace reading a fashion magazine. "Come to help?" she asked me.

"If you want. Why do you want to do the cooking? Jest's a good cook."

"And I'm not?"

"You're tops, but it's going to be work. There'll be writ-ers here and other guests from time to time."

"I want to keep busy," she said. "That Tony Scarpa's kind of a smart aleck, isn't he?"

"Big-city boy," I said. "You'll get to like him. He sure made a fool out of me in that ring today."

"*He* did?"

"Yup. He's fast, upstairs and down, thinks fast, moves fast. He could have had the welter title for years if he'd ever taken the game seriously."

I was standing near the sink and through the window above it, I saw the car come in the driveway and park, and Sergeant Sands get out of it.

I had the front door open by the time he got there and I brought him along with me back to the kitchen.

"Cup of coffee, Sergeant?" Sally asked him. "You look tired."

"I'll have a cup, thanks. I am tired." He nodded toward the living-room, and looked at me. "You've got some high-priced help in there."

"Nothing but the best for this one," I said. "Learn any-thing from that cabbie's girl friend, Sergeant?"

"Nothing. He didn't confide in her, it seems. And Bevilaqua's playing dumber than even he can be. That's where this thing revolves, back there in the *Hoot Owl Club;* that's the hub of this mess. But they'll give me nothing to go on. They're covering for somebody."

Sally brought him a cup of coffee, and he said, "Thanks." He smiled at her. Then he inspected the coffee cup as though there was something to see on it. There wasn't; it was a very ordinary cup.

I can't believe that he was embarrassed, but that's the way he looked. "So," he went on, "the only substantial suspect I have to go on, right now, is you. The chief's kind of annoyed about the way I've been riding with you. He wants me to crack down."

Chapter X

SALLY TOOK a deep breath. I took one, myself. I said, "It makes sense. If I was wearing your badge, I'd think just like the chief does."

"Except for the flesh on her teeth," he said. "Except for this—who was her boy friend at the party? Who brought her?"

"Wald would know that."

"He doesn't. He claims she wasn't even invited, by him. He doesn't even remember her coming in."

"You've questioned the other guests?"

"Hell, yes. The ones that didn't play dumb were dumb. Do you remember seeing her with anybody when you came in?"

"I don't remember anything but the windmill, Sergeant," I said.

"So." He shook his head. "Everybody trying to cover, Wald, Ruth Gonzales, Bevilaqua. I can't see Wald covering if he thought you were the killer. Because if he could prove that, you'd be vacating the title the hard way, and Giani's the logical successor. Or the logical winner in an elimination tournament. Wald would only cover if he knew you were innocent. And Wald's covering."

"And why would Harry Bevilaqua cover?"

"Not why, but *who*. Harry likes you, but he likes somebody else more. Who but the killer?"

"Harry liked Noodles, too."

"Sure. But that's a different kill. That's a professional kill. That's one may never get solved."

The picture of Johnny came to my mind, silent Johnny.

Sands said musingly, "Great stuff, conine. Soluble in alcohol. One of those Florida cops died the same way. Drinking man."

I saw Johnny standing in front of the door, and Sally waiting to get out. I said, "I can't seem to work up any sympathy for a Florida cop, but Noodles was kind of a nice little guy, despite the knife he pulled on me."

"Guys his size in his kind of company," Sands said, "almost have to carry a knife. That Gonzales woman is still crying."

Sally replenished the sergeant's cup. He looked at it again as he said, "Rumors are going around town. The wise guys seem to think this fight is in the bag." He sipped the coffee.

"That's logical enough, the terms we got out of them. It would look like we were selling the title. Only Max could keep them from the crown forever, and they know it. And they have to take our terms. They figure the title's worth it, I guess."

"It would be, to them. There's not much Pilgrim money around."

"There's my end of the purse, if anybody wants to cover it," I said.

The sergeant smiled, and stood up. "You sure are a confident man, Pilgrim. I'll ride with you awhile. Best thing about a job like mine, I don't mind losing it. Which the chief knows." He finished his coffee standing up. "You'll see a lot of me. I can find the door without help."

Seconds of silence, and Sally said, "I like him. He doesn't seem like a policeman at all."

"He does to me. I wonder if Harry Bevilaqua would tell

me anything he wouldn't tell the sergeant."

"He already has. I don't think he'd tell you any more, not after you blabbed to the law." She stood up. "You can help with dinner. There are some potatoes to peel."

I peeled spuds, and set the table and broke out the ice cubes for the drinking-water. Sound, muscle-building labor to ready me for my imminent and important defense of the title.

After dinner, the pinochle hounds went back to their battle, and I helped Sally with the dishes. It was eight o'clock when we finished, and it had been too much of a day for me. I couldn't keep my eyes open.

I fell asleep a few seconds after my head met the pillow and slept a dreamless sleep right through to dawn. And then came fully awake with the opening of my eyes.

Nobody was up, but I knew it wouldn't do me any good to stay in bed; I was as rested as it was possible to get. I got up quietly and put on the sweat pants and shirt and sneakers.

It was some day. The Pacific smooth as a blue lawn, the low clouds on its far rim pink in the morning sun. From the wet beach a sea gull looked at me curiously.

Easy, now, trotting the morning stiffness out of the leg muscles, sweating the sore edge of yesterday's labor out of my misused body, drinking in the salt air, blanking the mind.

Yesterday had taught me how far I was from my peak. Still, I'd been fighting right along, and better men than Tony Scarpa. The answer seemed to be I'd been fighting the same men over and over, men I'd watched in other bouts, men I knew. It was almost automatic, fighting men I knew as well as I knew Art Cary, Muggsy Ellis, and Charley Retzer.

And another thought came to me. I'd heard about fighters whose opponents had splashed without their knowing it; deals made by managers and one of the fighters, leaving the winner in the dark.

Had Max, I wondered, ever done that? No, not Max. But still, the way that Scarpa had scored on me—

Max and Sally were in the kitchen when I got back. Max was setting the table, and Sally was pouring popover batter into a muffin tin.

I had a small drink of water and sat near the biggest window. "That Scarpa sure got to me yesterday, Max," I said.

"Mmmmm-hmmm. He's got to plenty of them, in his time."

"I'm surprised I lasted this long," I said.

"Me, too," Max agreed. "Keep going; this fight isn't bad enough, you've got to work yourself into a mental lather. You want *me* to fight Giani for you?"

"If it would draw, I would. What are you nervous about?"

"Me—nervous? Why should I be nervous? You've got to fight him. How's that hand?"

"A little tender, that's all. Do you think that doctor knew his stuff?"

"No, he's a converted veterinary. He—"

"Stop quibbling, you two," Sally said sharply. "You haven't acted like this since the Robinson fight."

The last big one; the last one I'd worried about. I went over and kissed the back of her neck. She was wearing shorts and a halter and her perfume was light on the morning air.

"Easy, sailor," she said. "Max is watching."

"Jealous, that's Max," I said. "I trotted almost all the way to the seals. Aren't those seals screwy, Max?"

"Anti-Semitic bastards," he said. "They just looked right through me."

Charley Retzer came into the kitchen then, huddled

into a big sweater. "Isn't there any heat over that garage? Tony and I damned near froze last night."

Max smiled. "Go easy on Luke, and I'll show you how to turn on the furnace. Tony almost put him away with the big gloves yesterday."

"That's what I hear," Charley said. "Tony should have fought middleweight, huh?"

Annoyance in me. Ridiculous, of course, but there. I smiled.

"Or I should have had somebody in my corner besides that meat-head, Doc Heinrich, in Jersey City," Charley went on. "You've had some lucky nights, Champ."

I smiled, the burn growing in me.

"For instance," he continued, "you could have been fighting when Walker and Greb and Tiger Flowers were going. You'd have been fighting prelims for the Elks Club."

"Sure," I said.

"Or you could have had any other manager in the world but Max Freeman, and you'd be lucky to even—"

"Shut up!" Sally said.

We all looked at Sally. Her face was white, her blue eyes were blazing. She had a big mixing-bowl in one upraised hand, and it was ready for Charley.

"Lay off Luke," she said. "You fools don't know what you're doing."

Charley grinned. "Ahh, baby, the hell we don't. We're trying to bring out the old tiger in him. We're needling him for a purpose, kid."

"He doesn't need it. He's got pride, pride, *pride*. That's all he needs, and all he ever had."

Charley's voice was quiet. "As far as you know. You didn't know him when he had something else. The first time I fought him, I wanted to run and hide after the third round. That was before he got civilized."

"That's the way I like him," she said.

"You and Giani," Charley agreed. "Relax, Sal."

The hand holding the bowl trembled, and then the bowl fell to the floor and bounced along the tile. Sally put both hands to her face and her shoulders shook as she took a deep and noisy breath.

I put an arm around her. "Easy, kid. They're my friends, honey. It was all in fun."

"It wasn't fun for you. You know it wasn't. I was watching your face, and I knew it, too."

Charley looked at her coldly; Max snorted something and went out of the room. The side door opened, and Tony Scarpa came in.

"I smell something good," he said genially. His quick eyes moved from Charley to me and Sally. "And something bad," he added. "Lovers' quarrel?"

"The boys were needling me," I said. "Charley claims I'm Mr. Horseshoes."

"You've had a lot of breaks," Tony said easily, "but now you've got Giani. Into each life some rain must fall. When do we feed?"

Sally's composure was back. "In ten minutes."

It was a quiet meal, except for Tony. He voiced his opinions on this and that; he wasn't a man who needed any help to keep a conversation going.

Charley looked owly; Max's face was carefully blank. Jest ate quietly, in a world of his own. Luke Pilgrim, the cheese champ, said nothing, burning slowly.

I took on Charley that afternoon. I watched his feet and watched his eyes and seemed to know every punch he was going to throw before he threw it. Against Charley I looked good.

And he was trying. He had the memory of those last couple rounds of our bout and annoyance at Sally's interference this morning. He knew all my tricks and tip-offs;

he knew me like a son.

But he couldn't score consistently. In the clinches, my hands were always inside; in the corners, his back was always to the ropes. I kept him off balance. I kept on top of him and the pace of the sparring was my pace. I had him blowing at the final bell.

"I didn't earn my dough," he said. "I'm not in shape."

"You'll earn it before we're through," I told him.

He looked at me strangely. "Tough guy? Luke, I know you. Don't talk out of character."

Max said, "Want to try a round or two with Tony?"

"Hell, yes," I said.

Splat, splat, splat again. But not always scores. Some on my forearms, some on my gloves, some on the high shoulder. Moving in and moving out, hydraulic Tony Scarpa, smooth as new oil. But I didn't look like the complete bum, this time.

The bell, and I was conscious of spectators. Harry Bevilaqua was leaning against the trunk of the eucalyptus tree, missing nothing. Ruth Gonzales was with him.

Max took off the gloves, and Jest gave me a robe, and I went over to talk to Harry and the dead-eyed Ruth.

"Afternoon, Champ," Harry said. "That Tony can move, can't he?"

"He sure can. Good afternoon, Ruth."

She nodded, and looked away, staying close to Harry.

"You didn't look so good," Harry said.

"I looked worse yesterday against Tony. Remember, he's a welter, and fast."

"He's no welter no more, nor fast," Harry said. "You just didn't look good, Champ."

"Lay off, Harry," I said. "Did you come out here to heckle me?"

"No, just wanted to see you go. Want to know how to bet."

"Bet on Giani," I said. "You like him."

"I hear that's the bet," Harry said. Even voice, quiet.

I studied him a good five seconds. "What's on your mind, Harry?"

"What should be? Brenda dead, Noodles dead. You fighting Giani, and the word around it's in the bag. I'm just seeing for myself. Noodles was my friend."

"And Brenda wasn't?"

"Not like Noodles."

I said easily, "You know more about both murders than I do, Harry. Maybe I should be watching you."

"My place is open to the public."

"This isn't," I said. "Not today. Get out of here, Harry."

His big face puzzled, then set. "You mean that, Luke?"

"I mean it. If you want to play cop, get a badge, get a gun."

"I've got a gun," he said. "I don't need no badge. I'll go, if that's orders."

Then Max was there, and Max said, "What the hell's going on? What's the matter here?"

"The big meatball's threatening me," I said. "He's throwing his acreage around."

Tony Scarpa came over, and he talked rapid Italian to Harry, nothing I understood. Charley Retzer came, and Jest, and Ruth Gonzales began to cry.

I said, "I'm sorry, Ruth. I wasn't including you. You can stay as long as you want."

"I'll go," she said, and she had Harry's arm. "Come. We go."

Harry's smile was scornful. "I'll be ringside, Luke."

"I'll dump him in your lap," I said. "Beat it."

Max was in front of me. Tony said quietly, "Relax, Champ. Take it easy." Jest flanked Max, saying nothing.

Harry turned his huge back on us, and walked off with Ruth.

"Noodles," Tony said. "Noodles was his best friend.
Noodles was always in his corner, in the old days."

I was trembling and there was a touch of nausea in my
tight stomach. Jest put a limber black hand up and began
to massage the back of my neck.

"Save it," Jest said quietly. "Save it for Giani, for when
you get paid." His voice soft as his hands, his sleepy poise
soothing.

"What the hell got into that big wop?" Max said. "I
never knew he was that punchy."

"Noodles," Tony said again. "When do we eat?"

"What's Noodles got to do with Luke?" Max asked
him. "And what do you know about that, anyway?"

Tony winked at me. "We *Italians* confide in each other.
What's for supper, Max?"

"Noodles," Max said, "for you."

Sally was waiting on the drive in front of the house
when we came back. Her eyes searched mine, asking questions.

"I'm better," I said. "I'm beginning to shape up."

"What was Harry here for? What was the ruckus down
there?"

"Nothing, honey. I don't want to talk about it now."

"All right." Her bright eyes moving over my face. "*One*
more question—was that Ruth Gonzales with him?"

"Yes."

She took a deep breath. "I don't feel like cooking, tonight. Couldn't we all go to a restaurant? Couldn't you
and I go to a movie or something, Luke? Wouldn't that be
all right, Max?"

"I'll cook," Jest said. "I like to cook. There's plenty of
stuff to work with. We can eat here in a jiffy."

Sally was still looking at Max.

Max said, "Okay. A movie for you two. I want him in
bed by ten-thirty. We'll play pinochle. We'll be up." He

smiled at Sally. "Biggest fight of his life coming up."

"I know, Max," she said. "Don't worry about that, for a second. I know."

We ate at the restaurant next to the seal tank. We got some fish for the seals first, and watched them perform and then we went in and took a table overlooking the ocean.

It had turned into a gray day, and the ocean was dirty along here. It wasn't exactly an inspiring view today.

Lobster for Sally and scallops for me, and very little talk between us. Tired, Sally looked, and sad.

She sipped her coffee and I lighted her cigarette for her, and she looked out at the littered water as she said, "I'm sort of—frightened, Luke. Everything seems to be coming to a head. Tell me about Harry Bevilaqua now."

I told her. Over her shoulder I could see the seals watching the doorway, watching for somebody to come with a plate of fish, the always hungry seals, like Los Angeles sports writers.

When I'd finished, she said, "Why don't we go and talk to him? He's a reasonable man, Luke."

"He's not a reasonable man right now," I said. "I can't risk the hand again. I was lucky last time."

"Hit, hit, hit—" she said bitterly. "Is that all you know?"

"Until after the fight. I'll be all soft and tender again, after that. I'll be your lover boy again."

She put a hand on mine. "Sometimes I don't think you're for me at all. But then I think what it would be without you, and I shiver, Luke."

"I'm kind of a handsome bastard," I admitted.

"I'm glad you're *not* handsome," she said. "Are we going to live out here?"

"I'd like to."

"Some days like this, I loathe this country. It's so gloomy and littered and raw-looking."

"You're forgetting those Chicago Januaries," I said. "And that dirty south side and the stockyards and the wind off the lake."

"I suppose. And Colonel McCormick." She put her cigarette out in the ash tray, watching it as she asked, "Do you think of Brenda much?"

"I think of her. But I feel that I—didn't kill her, now. I'm like the big boy, I think about Noodles more."

"I think of Brenda," she said.

"Well, don't."

She looked up. ":Oh, not the way you think. I feel sorry for her. She was really trying to make it the hard way,' wasn't she?"

"All the ways are hard. We'd better find a cheerful movie."

It wasn't quite that, it was *A Streetcar Named Desire*. It was a fine job.

"But a long climb down from *Glass Menagerie*," Sally thought.

"I liked it better," I told her.

"You would. Rape, perversion, violence. That's too easy. *Menagerie* had subtlety and tenderness and depth. *Menagerie* had craftsmanship. Any hack can write violence and sex."

"I refuse to listen to your opinions when you won't listen to mine," I said. "Is there a motel near here?"

"You go to hell, Punchy. I thought I'd given you some discernment. I thought you were developing taste and balance and sensitivity."

"I'm trying," I told her, and took her hand. "But none of those will help me against Giani."

"And neither will a motel. What time is it?"

"Ten o'clock."

"We'll just about make it by ten-thirty. Max will be waiting."

"To hell with Max."

"And Patsy Giani? To hell with him, too?"

"Yes. He doesn't bother me."

"Not *much*, he doesn't. Let's get home, Champion."

Searchlights stabbing the sky, traffic moving on the wide streets, the Ford talking quietly to herself.

"Why," Sally asked, "couldn't you have been anything in the world but a fighter? You've some good stuff in you, Luke."

"If I hadn't been a fighter," I pointed out reasonably, "I wouldn't have known Max. I wouldn't have gone to that party in Chicago and met you. So what difference would it have made to you what I was?"

"We'd have met," she said.

"You don't believe that. You're too much of a realist."

"Me? You're the realist."

"Not me," I said. "I still believe in God."

"I'll bet. The crown, that's your God, the title, the top of the ant heap."

"Lay off," I said.

Silence, and then her hand came over to grip my knee. "I do it with my tongue and you do it with your fists. It's cleaner your way, isn't it? It's more dignified."

"I love you," I said, "disposition and all. Moods and attitudes and gray hair and fine figure and intellectual snobbery and underwear advertisements. Everything you do and are is exactly what I want. You can't help trying to make me over; that's the woman in you. I don't mind."

Nothing from her, her hand on my knee, no words of love from her; she wasn't as sure as I was at the moment.

Off Sepulveda, a supermarket and the bakery sign, the blue windmill revolving. Sally's grip tightened and relaxed.

Down to Olympic and Olympic through the tunnel, and out onto the Coast Highway. Black night, no stars in sight, no sound from Sally.

Tomorrow, I thought, *I'll plaster that Scarpa. I've got him figured now; I've got the rhythm of him. I'll get to him.*

Sally said, "I wish you could remember about Brenda."

"You don't wish it as much as I do." I was stopped for the light at Sunset, and I looked over at her. Her profile was toward me, her gaze directed through the windshield.

She took her hand from my knee and reached into her purse for a cigarette. She lighted it. "That Harry Bevilaqua's the key to the whole thing, isn't he? He knows."

"I think he does. Maybe he's next."

"And maybe he's *it*. Maybe he's the killer."

"Maybe."

"Of Brenda. And maybe Noodles, too. No, not Noodles."

The light changed, and I moved out in low gear. "No, not Noodles. You can chalk that one up to Johnny."

"I suppose. God, what a—thing he is."

Nothing from me. A sign read: *Slide Area Drive With Caution.* A huge rock had fallen from the cliffs above the road here and crashed into a garage of one of the beach cottages. It had completely demolished the garage. If it had chanced to hit the cottage, instead, it would have done as much for the cottage. And the sleeping occupants.

Design? Chance?

"What are you thinking about?" Sally asked.

"About that rock that fell the other day. Was it just chance it didn't hit the house?"

"What else could it be?"

"I don't know. I'm asking you. You're the bright one."

"It rained," Sally said patiently. "The rain eroded the cliff. The rock was dislodged. It fell. There was a garage in the way. If you're thinking of God, He didn't build the house or garage. If you believe in Him, He could have

put the rock there, and made it rain. He could have antici-
pated the people who were going to move there. But
wouldn't it be kind of stupid to believe He'd cause all the
damage that rain caused to thousands of people, just to
scare some family in Malibu with a rock that hit their
garage?" She chuckled.

"Don't make a federal case out of it," I said. "I get the
shivers, that's all, when I think of that rock. When I think
how all a man's lifetime of planning can be smashed by a
falling rock."

"Or a falling plane," Sally said, "or a falling star. Or
even a falling arch, if you're a mailman. You can't be
ready for *everything*, Luke."

"I guess not. Giani, I can be ready for. I'd better concentrate on that."

"It's more in your line. But *can* you be ready for him?"

"He can be hit. I hit pretty hard."

"So does he, I hear."

"Yes. Yes, indeed."

Silence for almost a mile. We passed the seal tanks, the
Topanga Road.

Then, as we turned into the winding driveway of the
estate, Sally said, "But you *have* to fight him, don't you?
You couldn't retire without fighting him, could you?"

"I have to fight him. You know it, and you know why."

"I know why, but you don't. Oh, I'm not going to talk
like that any more."

The floodlight that illuminated the parking-area was
on, and Tony Scarpa's bleached and battered station wagon was parked there.

"He's so smart and talented," Sally said. "Why isn't he
rich?"

"Relax," I said. "Tony's made a mint, in his time. Maybe he doesn't worship money."

"But *I* do? Is that what you're saying?"

"I don't want to fight," I told her. "I'm saving all my fight for Patsy."

Nothing from her. We walked along the parking-area to the lighted entryway, and I held the door for her, and she went through.

The boys were playing in the kitchen tonight. They all looked up and smiled, and Max said, "Good evening, love birds."

Chapter XI

I COULDN'T GET TO SLEEP that night. Too much had happened this past week. I felt crowded and edgy. Tomorrow was Sunday, and the scribes would be here, watching me work.

Why couldn't Sally and I get along? Why did we have to scratch at each other all the time? From the direction of the living-room, I heard Tony laugh.

Tony could always laugh, broke as he was. Maybe being broke is one of the requirements for laughter. And knowing you're good, knowing there isn't a man in your division you couldn't beat if you wanted to. And then not particularly wanting to.

I wondered how many deals Tony had made. And Charley? Charley had a rep as an honest fighter, but that Giani farce was too much to swallow.

I thought of Max, who'd been a happy man the past few years and was now getting more irritable by the minute. And Jest, with his soft, quiet poise. I thought of the soul-sick Ruth Gonzales, and I thought of Brenda Vane.

How many horizontal encounters had she had in that big bed with the maroon sheets? And in other beds and couches and davenports and parked cars and dark fields? For love or money, in loathing and ecstasy, in pain and peace. What she offered was a product constantly in demand, and she didn't ask for a lifetime contract.

Fighting, they say, is a cruel trade. Being a woman can be a crueler one, both ways. Man and woman, that was the real battle of the century, of *any* century.

Which brought me back to Sally, which would bring no sleep.

Harry Bevilaqua, Paul D'Amico, Sergeant Sands and Sergeant Nolan, Johnny, the landlady, the hotel clerk, Vickie and Vera, George and Sam Wald, Michael Lord, and the dead Noodles. The seals and the windmills. The windmills, a pair of them, went around and around and around and around—

A bright room and lassitude and the sound of water. Even in the better California homes, you can always hear the water in the pipes. Maybe the pressure is too high, or the pipes too small, but you can always hear the water.

I heard Sally talking quietly to Max, right outside my door. "Why not let him sleep?"

"I'm awake," I called. "I'll be up and out pretty soon."

Dopey, dead, weary. A warm shower and then cooler, but it didn't help much. An ache in the knees, a tiredness in the shoulders, a defeat in the mind.

Fruit juice and milk and eggs. Tony and Charley gabbled; the rest of us were quiet.

Charley asked me, "You want us to pull 'em, today, Luke? You want us to miss?"

"You won't need to," I said.

"We don't want to make you look bad in front of the customers," Tony said. "I hear some local pride is coming in for a couple rounds, too."

I looked at Max.

"Royal Lincoln," Max said.

A hitter, and a light-heavy, a Negro lad who could wallop.

"Kind of early for that, isn't it?" I asked.

"Never too early to know," Max said. "You can always

sprain an ankle or something."

"He's way past his peak," Charley said. "He's out of shape."

Scarpa chuckled. "Sure, and he hits like Max Baer used to. Don't forget to duck, Luke. Or let Charley go with him."

"He'd be too much for Charley," I said. "And you, too, Tony. I'll handle him."

Tony chuckled again and shook his head. Charley's face showed nothing.

It was the kind of day Sunday should be, clear and warm, and we drew a good crowd. I didn't go up against Tony; just Charley and the black boy, Royal Lincoln. Charley opened the show.

He didn't miss a trick, butting, thumbing, heeling me, clowning, clinching, switch hitting.

In the middle of the second, in the clinch, I told him, "Don't get too cute, Charley."

He put a shoulder into my chin, and shoved.

I found his right foot with my left, clamped it down, and slammed a hook in under the ribs. He started to crowd me, and I backed off and caught him with a clean right hand on the break.

A murmur went through the crowd, and the bell rang.

Jest was smiling, wiping off my face. Max was over talking to Charley.

"Charley must have gone crazy," I said. "What's his angle?"

Jest said quietly, "D'Amico's out there. Maybe Max wants to show him we're ready for anything."

"The less we show D'Amico, the better," I said.

Jest shrugged, toweling my shoulders, the back of my neck, my chest. I turned to look over the crowd.

Two rows deep all around the ring, and some standing in small groups farther out. One group of two seemed to be apart from the others in more ways than one; Paul D'Amico and his silent partner, Johnny.

For a second, our eyes met, and D'Amico smiled. He made no gesture, but the smile was smug enough to tell me he wasn't worried about a thing. This was another in the D'Amico bag.

Then Charley was coming across toward me, and grinning, and I felt cold and steady and calloused.

It was a dull round, a round of reflexes and counterpunching, a tired replay of a melody we'd worn thin through the years.

Under the eucalyptus tree, Royal Lincoln waited patiently.

He looked slow. He kept moving, though, hitting from a fairly square stance, erect and flat-footed. His right was carried high, but wide of his chin; the two early times he threw it, I could see it coming as slow as a balloon.

The third time, he almost knocked off my headguard.

I went into the ropes, and felt it again, an overhand right, a sucker punch. Had my eyes gone bad?

I could hear the murmur in the crowd through the buzzing in my ears. I could feel his bulk crowding me into a corner, and I put my hands inside, and burned my back on the ropes, trying to slide out.

He clubbed me again, and the redness came, and I poured leather like a Golden Glover, as he covered, riding it out.

The crowd was noisy, now, a fight crowd, and I'd driven Lincoln to the center of the ring. I was hitting him with both hands, but no place where it would hurt. He was covered; he didn't open up to strike back.

The rest of it was dull. The rest of it looked like Royal was under orders.

The scribes wanted to know about that overhand right; how much had it hurt?

"Plenty," I said. "Royal can hit." Local boy.

"Not like Giani," one of them said.

"Don't talk like a tourist," I told him. "Royal's always been one of the heaviest hitters in the business."

Some laughs. Except for a reporter from the *L. A. Times*.

It wasn't funny to him. He said stiffly, "I've heard Royal described as the heaviest hitter of all time."

"So have I," the other said, "but only in your column." Laughs.

Chinning with the crowd, making with the good will, building the gate. Fun in the afternoon sun, but the sun went down after a while, and they left, and it got cold.

"You sure stunk," Max said. "What the hell is it?"

"I don't know," I said. "The murders, I suppose."

"D'Amico starting to scare you?"

"Hell, no!" Why the "hell," why so emphatic? Was he?

"You're getting to be a regular gentleman," Max said. "Even when you foul, you do it in a nice, clean way. Sally's made a gentleman out of you."

"Maybe. Don't worry about it, Max. The worse I look, the more D'Amico will bet. The more he bets, the more he'll get hurt. And that's what you want, isn't it?"

"Gawd," Max said. "He ain't going to be hurt at all, the way you're going. But you are, bad."

"I'll be hurt," I agreed, "but I'm not going to lose, even if I have to carry an ax in there with me."

"You can't carry an ax," Max said. "That's the hell of it."

A hundred and sixty million people in this country and only I believed in me.

After supper the pinochle game started, and Sally and I sat in the big kitchen, playing canasta. Five minutes of that and she threw her cards, face up, on the table.

"Let's go to the *Hoot Owl Club*."

"Why? What can we learn there?"

"I want to talk to Ruth. She'll talk to me. She needs a friend, the way she must be feeling."

"She's got one," I said, "Harry the horse."

"I want to talk to him, too."

"Sally," I said patiently, "he's nobody to talk to, right now. And Ruth probably isn't, either."

"I'll go alone, then," she said. She stood up. "I want to know, Luke. All you care about is the title, but I want to know about that night."

"All right," I said. "God damn it, *all right!*"

She drove; she handled all of it. She told Max we were just going over to see some friends in Santa Monica, and she drove the car.

A damn-fool idea and I rode next to her in silence. Wisps of fog drifted over the highway from the beach side; the headlights of approaching cars were haloed by it.

Lincoln Boulevard was jammed with coming-home traffic, but was reasonably clear on our side. Not a word from either of us on the entire trip.

When we parked in the small parking-lot, we could hear the juke box going inside, and the sound of Harry's laugh. He must be feeling better.

The place was doing a business. Workingmen in their bright Sunday sport shirts and part-rayon slacks. Workingmen and their girls and wives. At the far end of the bar, Ruth Gonzales was sitting in front of a beer.

And next to a man, a small man with black, shiny hair and a garish sport shirt and an "Oh, yeah?" sort of look.

Her eyes met mine, then Sally's, and went back to the beer in front of her. Shamed, had she looked?

We crowded in at a spot not too far from them, and Harry came down to serve us.

His face blank. "What'll it be, folks?"

"A smile," Sally said. "When did you stop smiling, Harry?"

"When Noodles died. What'll it be, folks?"

I said, "You're judging us awful God-damned quick, Harry."

Next to me, a man said, "Hey, mister, there's ladies present."

"That's right," Harry said. "You owe the man an apology, Luke."

Redness in the mind, tremble in the hands. Sally's grip digging into my forearm. "He's right, Luke. You do owe the man an apology."

I turned to him and said, "I'm sorry. I apologize to both of you."

Beyond him, the woman he was with looked straight ahead, miffed. A heavy woman, heavily made up, her face blank in cheap pseudo-dignity.

Harry said, "That's better."

The man mumbled something and turned away.

Sally said, "I guess we shouldn't have come. Harry's the kind of moron who hates a fact." She took a breath. "Let's go, Luke."

"I'm here now," I said, "and Harry owes us more than silence."

The man next to me said, "Easy, mister. Let me warn you, fair, that big boy used to be murder in a ring."

"I know," I said. "I saw him murdered. I'll take a glass of milk, Harry. I don't know what Sally wants."

"A glass of beer," Sally said. "Eastern beer."

"You'll have to buy a bottle. I ain't got Eastern beer on tap."

"I can swing it," she said. "You know Luke had nothing to do with what happened to Noodles, Harry. You aren't so clean, yourself."

"Don't worry about me," he said. He turned to me. "I talked to Krueger yesterday. He got bounced, didn't he? Why?"

"How do I know? Sam Wald's the new manager. You tell me why. You're the man with answers."

"Krueger says it's a job, a job to end all jobs. He said millions are going to be bet on Giani. He said it's arranged all the way around. That puts you in the wrong kind of company for me."

"This place clear, Harry?" I asked him.

"Clear enough. Why?"

"You want to bet it against my end of the purse? You never had better odds. You can even keep the owl, for luck."

For seconds, he said nothing. "You're leveling, Champ?"

"Name me *one* time when I didn't."

He took a deep breath. "Yeah, that's right. Yes. Yes." He clicked his teeth. "I'll get the drinks."

The man next to me said, "Champ? Luke? Are you Luke Pilgrim?"

"That's right."

Nothing more from him. Harry came with a bottle of Milwaukee beer and a carton of milk and two glasses.

He set them down in front of us. "We all know who killed Noodles, don't we? Even the cops know."

"Johnny."

"Sure, and I thought you were working with those boys now. The way Krueger talked—"

"In a corner," I said, "very few guys know more than Dutch Krueger. Outside of his corner, I'm surprised he knows enough to find his way home."

"I guess. That's right, I guess. That's what they all say. But that Johnny, and what can we do about it? Even the cops can't do anything about it."

"What do you want to do about it?"

"I want to kill him."

"That wouldn't bring Noodles back. Get all the Giani money you can handle, Harry. You can buy a new owl, a platinum one."

"Oh, Champ," he said. "Jesus, Champ, maybe it's the way you feel, but— Oh, hell, it's the way I felt before the Burke fight, too."

"Hey, mister," Sally said, "there's ladies present."

Harry started to chuckle, and then he threw back his head, and the laugh came. On his perch, the owl shivered, and the blaring juke box seemed to whisper.

At the end of the bar, Ruth Gonzales watched him, and then she looked our way, and her gaze went to Sally, and she smiled.

The man next to us and his heavy-faced woman climbed off their stools, and Sally beckoned to Ruth. She came over, bringing the patent-leather kid along.

He was a jockey. His name was Ralph. He'd won eight in the last two days, out of eleven rides. He was hot.

Sally waited until he went to the growler to tell Ruth, "He's cute."

"He's all right," Ruth said. "He's no Noodles." Her voice was shaky. "They—the law, they still think I—had something to do with what happened."

"Have you any idea how it happened, Ruth?"

She shook her head. "I know he—knew something about the murder of that Brenda Vane." She lowered her voice, and looked down toward where Harry was serving some-one else. "And Harry does, too, I'm almost sure. But if he doesn't want to talk about it, I suppose I shouldn't."

"I wish you would talk about it, Ruth," Sally said gently.

Ruth shook her head. "I like both you kids. But Harry's my best friend in the world, and with him it's clean."

Then Harry was standing there, smiling at us. "Trying to pump her, you two?"

I nodded.

"Trouble," he said quietly, "always trouble with you, Luke."

"I want to know I didn't kill her," I said.

"You didn't. I know you didn't."

Next to me, Sally made a sound in her throat. I stared at Harry, waiting for what was coming.

His big face was composed. "As long as you know that, it doesn't matter to you who did, does it?"

"You mean," I asked, "you know who killed her, you know for sure?"

"I didn't say that, but it could be true. All I'm telling you is that you didn't kill her. I'm not admitting anything beyond that."

"He's a friend of yours, Harry?"

"I didn't say it was a 'he.' You're making noises like a cop, Luke."

"Maybe," I said, "if I knew who killed her, I'd remember what happened, in her apartment. Maybe I was there when the killer was."

"You weren't. Look, Luke, two guys besides the killer knew who killed her, *maybe*. One of them was Noodles, and he tried to get to you, *maybe*, after he learned he was poisoned. Johnny killed him, and that's not much of a 'maybe.' The boys who pull the strings on Johnny don't want you to know you're in the clear. They could get a title fight easier if you didn't know. And they could get you to throw the fight." He paused. "Maybe."

"Sergeant Sands knows I went to her apartment," I said. "I told him that, the other day. He says I didn't kill her. So there's no pressure on me from D'Amico. I wanted that fight, Harry."

He smiled, both big hands on the bar. "Okay, you got it. And what do you want from me?"

"Another glass of milk," I said, "and whatever the others are having they can have on me."

Ruth said, "Sally and I will have a bottle of champagne. That's what she had last time."

Sally nodded, her eyes still on Harry. "Don't you want to tell us all you know, Harry?"

"I don't and I won't," he said. "What'll you have, Ralph?"

"I can go for that champagne, too," he said.

Sally still watched Harry. "Was it her boy friend?"

·"Get her out of my hair, Luke," Harry said. "Get her off my back."

"She's jealous," I said. "She wants to know what happened."

"How do I know?" he said. "I'm no peeping Tom." He went down to get the champagne.

There was no more talk about the murder; Harry wouldn't have it. We talked of fights and horses and Harry Truman, under the watchful eyes of the stuffed owl. We talked about Paul D'Amico and Sam Wald and Patsy Giani and Johnny.

Harry said, "I'd like to have the four of them, right here in this room. Just you and me against the four of them, Luke."

"You could have Patsy," I said, "all by yourself."

Then Sally said, "Luke, it's ten o'clock."

We said good-by all around and they wished me luck, and we went out into the cold night.

As we walked to the car Sally said, "You drive. I think I'm drunk."

´I opened the door for her, and closed it, and went around to climb in behind the wheel.

As I pulled out onto Lincoln Boulevard, she said, "Glass menagerie."

"Come again?"

"Ruth and her little men, a glass menagerie, sort of. She wants to mother them. Or is that incestuous?"

"I don't know. I'm no peeping Tom. I wonder who killed Brenda. I wonder if I ever knew."

Sally didn't answer. Her head was back against the cushions, her eyes were closed.

Drifting fog and shrouded lights, the Ford perking in the damp air. Harry knew the killer, and I wondered if I did, too, if it was a mutual friend.

Maybe it was Harry.

Together, Harry and Noodles could have cooked up the tale about Brenda phoning, and fed it to me. But Noodles would know it wasn't true, and Harry might wonder.

No, not Harry; Noodles had been his friend, if Tony Scarpa was right on that.

But Tony might be Harry's friend, too, and—

It wasn't my baby. There were ten thousand cops in this town, trained in police work. I was no cop and not bright enough to make like one without the training.

Through the fog, the windmills came tilting at me and I saw the glass eyes of Harry's stuffed owl. That was the first time the owl had accompanied the windmills. Was there something churning in the unknown me, some message trying to get out of the void in my memory?

Sally said quietly, "What are you thinking about?"

"About my subconscious mind."

"Unconscious," she corrected me. "Something came out of it?"

"The owl is with the windmills now."

"Have another reefer," she said, and fell silent again.

Harry had stuck his neck out, admitting he knew I hadn't killed Brenda. Why had he done that? To take the heat off me, to put me in mental shape to meet Giani? That was very possible, once he believed there was no fix. He must want to see Giani get beat, after what happened to Noodles.

Damn it, I was no cop.

But involved in mankind, Luke Pilgrim, like it says in the quote in that book you never finished reading.

But windmills, what sense did windmills make? My head began to throb, and the Ford wandered across the double white line, and from nowhere headlights pounced at me.

I heard the shriek of tires as I pulled sharply to the right, and a woman's scream and a man's shouted curses.

"Luke, for God's sake—" Sally whispered.

The Ford still perking, the double white line where it belonged, the other car safely past.

"I must have dozed," I said. "You're all right? You didn't get bumped or anything?"

"I'll be all right as soon as I can swallow my heart. We were never so close to whatever's beyond, mister."

Bitterness in my mouth, and I slowed to a crawl, hugging the right side of the road, under the bluff.

She chuckled. "I just thought of a gag. You'll be the death of me yet."

Chapter XII

THE NEXT DAY was the red-letter day. I got to Scarpa. I got the pattern of him, the rhythm of him, and I plastered him. I nailed him sliding in and pasted him stumbling out and caught him in a corner for the first time since we'd tangled.

Either he was looking awful bad, or I was getting better.

"Off your feed?" I asked him. "Or too much pinochle, maybe?"

"You're better," he said. "Something's off your mind, too, isn't it? You look all business, for a change."

There was a small crowd there, and a few scribes. One of them said, "That's one hell of a change since yesterday. Of course, Tony's no Royal Lincoln, are you, Tony?"

Tony smiled. "He's a lot heavier."

Then, along the path from the garage, Royal Lincoln came moving leisurely, wearing a white robe, trimmed in scarlet, wearing his impassive, professional blandness.

I looked over to where Max was talking to a pair of scribes and caught his eye.

"Two rounds," Max called over. "In a couple minutes."

Tony said, "Move in on him, Luke. Don't let him use his reach."

"And keep your chin buried," the writer kidded me. "It would look bad in the papers if Royal tagged you."

Royal didn't tag me, not today. I kept an eye on that

high right hand when we were apart, but we weren't apart much. I moved under the right and hooked him silly, the first round.

The second round he played turtle, hiding behind his elbows and forearms, moving into a half-crouch.

He's too tall to do that against a man my size. I brought a couple of right hands up from the floor and we went back to yesterday's minuet.

Twice, he started that overhand right; both times, I beat him to the punch. It would be unfair to Western Union to say he telegraphed it; it was more in the nature of a night letter.

Royal Lincoln, as Charley had said, was a long way from his peak. But yesterday he had got to me with that prelim haymaker.

Maybe Harry Bevilaqua had done me more good than I'd realized last night.

Which I told Sally later.

"Whose idea was it, going to see Harry?" she asked.

"Yours."

"Well?"

"Well enough. You know, I haven't been this ready for years. I should taper off or I'll go stale."

"Max will decide that," she said.

Max said, "You're better, but not good enough. I want you nastier."

That seemed to be Charley's department. Charley got cute, hard to get to, a gloved butterfly. Making me miss, in front of the crowds, clowning it, drawing the laughs. No chance to counterpunch; he offered no leads. He didn't have to look good; no part of the gate was his.

Thursday, I told Max, "Not today, not Charley. He knows me too well. He's not that good and I'm not that bad. He just knows me too well."

"If you can't get to him," Max said, "what'll you do

against Patsy?"

"Patsy has to come to me, you know that. He can't win the title on a bicycle. I can hold it on a bike, but he can't win it. He's the *challenger*."

Max smiled. "Today, pretend Charley's the champ and you're the challenger."

I knew they were needling me but knowing it didn't help enough. I don't like to be laughed at. It's a thing a man has to learn, I know, but I'd never learned it.

Edgy, I got, even with Sally. She didn't sulk about it. I wish she had. She smiled her superior smile as though she was above this adolescent nonsense. She didn't snap back or sulk. She just smiled.

Sergeant Sands came, bringing Nolan along. They were getting nowhere. Everything revolved around Bevilaqua like spokes around a hub, but they were getting nowhere. They couldn't stay with it forever; this was a big town. And how was I getting along?

"If I don't die of my own poison, I'll make it," I told them.

Sands looked sadly thoughtful. "D'Amico's unloading bales of the green, and all on Giani," he said.

"Get some."

"That's straight? I could use a newer car."

"Anything you lose, I'll match. Get some of that Giani money."

Nolan said, "Intent won't win it, Champ. They don't pay off on trying."

"They'll carry one of us to the stool," I said. "I figure it will be Giani."

Nolan shrugged. "Giani figures it the other way. All the smart boys are figuring it his way."

"I've said all I'm going to say," I told them. "You'll have to decide for yourselves how smart the smart boys are."

Sands grinned and stood up. "Okay, Champ. I shouldn't say it, being from Homicide, but I hope you murder him."

All this time, I hadn't seen Giani. Pictures of him in action I'd seen until I was dizzy and the memory of the fights I'd seen him in was with me, night and day. But Patsy, in the flesh, I hadn't seen since we'd signed for the fight.

I saw him for the first time at the weighing-in. He looked about eighteen years old, pink and hard and ready.

He was a quarter pound under the limit; I was a half.

He said, "I've been living for this day."

I said nothing. I saw the hitting muscles in his sloping shoulders, the easy way he moved, the poise that screamed confidence—and for the first time I wasn't so certain I could do it.

No pug ever realized he was past his peak until he was *way* past it. There wasn't any reason why I should be different. Or any reason for me to be sure I could take this young mixer if I was at my peak.

Tony and I went back to Hollywood to a hotel. Max and Jest went out to the arena to check over the dressing-room and the ticket sale.

Tony wasn't talkative for a change. I lay on the davenport; he sat near the front windows, reading a *Racing Form*.

I stared at the ceiling and listened to the traffic, remembering how Giani had looked on the scales, not a soft spot in that pink hide, not a worry showing on that square face.

"How you betting, Tony?" I asked.

"I wouldn't bet against you, Champ. I hope you win."

"Because of D'Amico?"

"That's part of it. What a name for a son-of-a-bitch like that, 'D'Amico.' "

"It means something?"

"In Italian, it means 'friend.' Some friend, huh?"

"He's a friend to Johnny. What does Scarpa mean?"

"Shoe. That's me, soft-shoe Tony Scarpa."

"And Bevilaqua?"

He told me, and that was it. That was the link, the tie-up. That gave the windmills meaning, and all the rest of it. That's why she was alone at the party.

I went to the phone and called the *Hoot Owl Club*. Harry wasn't there. Ruth was. I told her, "Have him phone me as soon as he comes in." I gave her the number of the hotel.

' Sergeant Sands wasn't at the station, either, and I left the same message.

When I'd finished making the second call, I turned to find Tony staring at me. "What the hell goes on?"

"I know who killed Brenda Vane now," I said.

"You think you know—or you know?"

"I'm damned near sure."

He looked at me quietly. "Well, to hell with it. First the fight. You can't think of anything but the fight now. You're going to need your moxie for this one."

I went back to the davenport. I stretched full length. "I know, I know." I stared at the ceiling and went back to that morning Max had been eating corn in the suite. I added up the incidents since, the things that had seemed meaningless at the time but took on meaning through the new focus.

The phone rang, and I started to get up, but Tony said, "Got it."

"Hello," he said, and "Who is this, Sally? Okay." He smiled at me. "This one you can have."

Her voice was tight. "Luck, Luke. I can't watch it, I've decided. Is it important to you that I watch it?"

"I'd rather you didn't," I said. "I don't want to reveal that side of me. Where'll you be?"

"The same hotel. I've got the suite you and Max had.

That place in Malibu was too big to be alone in. Luke, how do you feel?"

"As ready as I'll ever be. I've a lead on the murder. Tony gave it to me. I phoned Sergeant Sands, but he wasn't in."

"You're serious?"

"I'm serious. I don't want to talk about it now. I'm not in a position to."

From his chair Tony laughed. "Tell her I'm here. I might squeal."

"Luke, for heaven's sakes, don't talk so mysteriously. Who, what is it— Who killed her, Luke?"

"I'm not sure," I said, "and as Tony told me, it's nothing to fret about *before* the fight. I'll see you as soon as I can. I've got to see some people after the fight, but I'll get to you first second I can."

Silence for seconds. Then: "Luke, are you in danger?"

"Only from Giani. I'll see you, darling." I hung up.

Tony was back to the *Racing Form*. I went back to the davenport. I said, "Don't you want to know, Tony?"

He looked at me and shrugged.

"You *know* who killed her, don't you?" I said. "At least you've got a hunch."

"I might have a hunch. So what? That's not my business."

"Murder should be everybody's business."

"Cut it out, Luke. Thousands of people are murdered every year, and you never gave any of them a second thought. This one was close to you, so we're all supposed to be concerned. To hell with it; I'm no cop. And I don't like most of the cops I've met."

"Met many?"

"Dozens."

"I'm glad I'm not like you, Tony."

"Huh. Same here. If it's who I think it is, I'm sorry

you found out, if you did. What was the girl? A tramp. D'Amico's gun kills a poor little punk, and do you worry about him? No, you're not concerned. You're not involved, so you're not concerned. But you give with the platitude about murder being everybody's business. You can get awful stuffy at times, Luke."

"I worry about Noodles," I said. "And I hate D'Amico as much as you do. You do hate him, don't you? You try to play it easy and light, but in *your* trade, you don't want any D'Amicos."

"I guess that's right."

"Would you help me with that?"

"With D'Amico? Sure. With the other, no. But with D'Amico, sure. You got an idea, or something?"

I had some ideas, which I told him.

When I'd finished, he said, "Did your memory come back, or are you just guessing all this?"

"I'm guessing. It all makes sense, though."

He took a deep breath. "It sure as hell is a dumb time for you to be thinking of anything but the fight."

"All right," I said. "You see Harry, and you talk to Sergeant Sands. Rent a room here and have them change my calls to that room. I'll show you how much I'm fretting; I'll take a nap."

"I'll bet you will, at that," he said. "You're sure disciplined."

Sally called it "cold" and Max "nasty" and Tony "disciplined." A very discerning gent, this Tony.

He said, "We don't need to rent a room. I'll take the phone here. I'll tell the operator to give us a short ring. I want to see you sleep. This, I can't miss."

"What's so remarkable about being able to sleep?"

He didn't answer. He grinned at me, and sat down near the phone. I stretched out, seeing the windmills, which now made sense. The void was still there, and might always be to my conscious mind. But out of the unconscious, out of the chained memory cells, this pair of symbols had tried to point to a murderer.

The windmills turned lazily. The seals stretched their necks. Max ate corn in a bright Beverly Hills suite. I dozed.

I heard Max's voice, later, and Tony's, but they were pitched too low for me to make out anything they said.

When I wakened, Max was in the room's only big chair, watching me. Tony wasn't in sight.

"Everything all right?" I asked him.

"My end's being handled fine. And yours?"

"Ready as I'll ever be. Where's Tony?"

"You tell me. What are you two cooking up? What's it all about?"

"I'll tell you later, Max. You're too excitable to know anything about it before the fight."

He looked at me a while, then stood up and went over to the window. His back was to me now. He said nothing.

"I'd better eat," I said. "What time is it?"

"Four o'clock."

"A steak," I said, "and a salad. That it, Max?"

"Why ask me? What am I to you?"

I came over to put an arm around his shoulders. "My best friend. After I draw and quarter this Patsy and take care of a few minor matters, we'll settle down, Max. We'll go into the used-car business. Foolish Freeman and Loony Luke, the craziest traders in town. We'll have a neon sign thirteen stories high and two solid blocks of used Cadillacs. I'll marry Sally and we'll pick up a used movie star for you and we will go Hollywood, but big. It's going to be great."

"Bull. What are these 'minor matters' you mentioned? Is murder one of them? Is D'Amico? Luke, that kind of stuff is out of your line. You're not tough enough for that."

"I was the third toughest guy in the All Saints choir," I said. "Let's get the steak. And maybe a small snifter for you."

He put an arm around me, and squeezed. "Damn you. You son-of-a-bitch. All right, let's go. But we're not eating here. This is no day for a crummy hotel steak. I know a place."

The place was on "restaurant row" otherwise known as La Cienega, and the steak was up to the Freeman standard, as was the salad and the service.

The only thing not up to Max's standard was Max. He was unhappy. No oral complaints, not another word about D'Amico, just the silent sadness.

Then, as we paid the check, he said, "You haven't seen the arena yet. We ought to go out, while it's still light. Twenty thousand people, it will hold. *Twenty* thousand."

"Migawd," I said, "the Garden only holds eighteen thousand."

"Sure. That's why they stretched this one. C'mon, I want to show you how crazy this town is getting on sports."

It was some spot. Of glass brick and stainless steel, triangular in shape, the box-office apex of the triangle on the corner of Moorpark and Fulton, in Sherman Oaks. The parking-lot would hold six thousand cars.

There were electric-eye calculators to measure the traffic flow into the parking-lot, there were replicas of the gadgets at each of the entrances to the arena. The soft drinks and hot dogs, the programs and souvenirs, the cigarettes and cigars could all be bought from machines in the lobby.

"It gives me the shivers," I said. "Everything's mechanical."

"Right," Max said. "Everything but the fighters. Now if we could get a robot to fight Giani—"

The dressing-rooms were too new to have any odor but

damp plaster. They were underground, serviced by esca-
lators, equipped with built-in infrared lamps and air-
cushioned massage tables, with a medical center completely equipped for emergency surgery.

We went from the medical rooms to the plush offices behind the Moorpark ticket office. Paneled in etched ply-
wood, furnished in splashy colors, carpeted in sea-green
nylon frieze.

We went out into the lobby from the last office, and two
men were standing there, talking.

Sam Wald and Paul D'Amico.

They both looked up, and Sam smiled. "Ready to go,
Luke?"

"I've never been readier," I said. "Some place you've
got."

D'Amico said, "I've been trying to phone you, Luke.
I'd like a word with you." He looked at Max and back at
me. "Alone."

I grinned at him and shook my head.

"Scarpa talked to me," he said. "He told me you wanted
to talk to me."

"Not *before* the fight, Paul. This one I want. I hope you
haven't bet more than you can afford to lose."

A door marked *Gentlemen* which led to the lobby, now
opened, and Johnny came out. His eyes moved over all of
us, sizing up the tableau. It would take labeling, I thought,
to identify Johnny as a gentleman.

Sam Wald's smile was gone. Next to me, Max was silent.
D'Amico said, "Don't make any serious mistakes, Luke."

I shook my head. "Be seeing you, boys."

Outside, Max said, "You fool, you damned fool. Do you
have to antagonize him?"

I turned to face the glass and shining steel, the glittering
arena that should have been a monument to the game, but
was only a symbol of the racket. Triangular was the right

shape for it; it had been built by angles.

"Take a good look at it," Max said, "and think of the money *you're* trying to buck."

"Guys like us built the damned thing, Max. Without us, and the other athletes, there'd be no stadiums, no sport pages; half the colleges in the country would fold up. And Paul D'Amico would be selling bananas."

"And what would Johnny be doing?"

"Pimping, I suppose. Or peddling dirty postcards."

"I wish I could be as dumb as you are," Max said sadly. "I don't remember ever being that dumb. Is it because Johnny's *small* that you're not scared of him?"

"I'm scared of him, but he'll be in the clink before the night's over, Max. Let's talk about something else."

We didn't talk. We went back to the hotel and picked up Tony and Charley, and Max and I went with them while they ate. Then we picked up Jest and went back to the arena.

The place was starting to fill up and it was a half hour to the first prelim.

"Some house we'll have, Max," I consoled him.

"Taxes will eat it up," he said. "Who can make money, today?"

In the dressing-room, a couple scribes were already waiting. One of them asked, "Got an opinion on it, Champ?"

"I'll win," I said. "Probably by a TKO."

He smiled. "One of those, huh?"

"If he starts it. It'll be clean as long as he keeps it clean."

"You wouldn't want us to quote that."

"No. No, just say he is a clean and red-blooded young American and he has earned his chance at the highest award his field offers. Say that it will be a clean and honest affair and I sincerely hope the better man wins." I sat on the rubbing-table. "Personally, I intend to murder the son-of-a-bitch."

"He likes you, too," the other reporter said. "He's really been aching for this one, hasn't he?"

"That's what I hear. I don't know the man socially."

There were other reporters, after that, as the prelims went on. I undressed, and Max brought over my trunks and shoes. And the supporter—with the cup in it.

"You'll need the cup tonight," Max said. "I should get a barbed one."

Two could play that game, too. I got up onto the rubbing-table, and Jest began to dig at me, humming to himself in a low, melodious voice.

Max told Charley, "You'd better get on the door now. I don't want to let in anybody but top brass. The semi's on."

In a corner, Tony held up a pail. "Take a look at it; it's worth seventy-five bucks. That's what ringside's bringing."

I looked at Max. "That's not true?"

"First three rows," Max said. "We can keep the whole administration in mink coats."

A title fight, in a sports-hungry town, in a town that really promotes. Jest worked me over and then I sat up, and Max wrapped my hands, taking his time, careful and slow and snug.

Jest was digging the back of my neck, humming, and Max was lacing my shoes, when the door opened, and Sergeant Nolan came in.

He looked at Max and Tony and inclined his head toward the door. "Outside."

Max looked at him blankly, as Tony headed for the door. Max said, "You're out of line, Sergeant. There aren't enough cops on the force to separate me from this boy right now."

"Please, Max," I said. "It's okay. The sergeant is just rough by training. He means well."

"I'll give him a minute," Max said, "and then I'll have

the chief in here. He's out in that crowd." He went out.

Nolan said, "What the hell are you cooking up? If you know who the killer is, tell us. The department doesn't go in for amateur theatricals."

"I don't know who the killer is," I told him. "I've got a big hunch, and if we work like Scarpa told you we wanted to, maybe we'll nail him. It's nothing to me, either way. Suit yourself."

"You mean you're not naming any names? What if something happens to you?"

"All right. I'll name a name, in return for your promise we work it like it was outlined to you. You see, I want somebody besides Brenda Vane's killer. I want Johnny, and I think D'Amico will give him to us."

"D'Amico give us Johnny? Are you crazy?"

"Maybe. How far have you guys got with D'Amico or Bevilaqua? I guarantee you I'll get further with Bevilaqua."

The door opened, and Max said, "Do I get the chief?"

Nolan looked at me, and I leaned over to whisper a name in his ear. He stared at me, frowning, and then took a deep breath. "Okay, Pilgrim. Okay. Sands is sold on you, anyway. This was my idea."

He went out, and Max and Charley and Tony came in. Max locked the door. "I wonder how that lame-brain's going to like his beat in Venice."

Jest went back to rubbing my neck and humming. Tony and Charley picked up pails. Max brought the robe over.

His face was sad, and his voice. "Okay, baby, it's time. That flat-footed bastard, screaming in at a time like this."

Jest said, "We don't worry, do we, Champ? This one we got. Every dime I own in the world is riding on this one."

I smiled at him. "You're the only man in the room betting on me, Jest."

"I'm the only man in the room that knows," he said.

"We go. Now, we go."

Now, we go. Out into the deserted hallway and over to the moving escalator, and up, Max and Jest and I and the two free-loaders.

Slowly upward into the rear apex of the big triangle, and the long aisle stretching down to the ring. The joint was jammed.

Patsy was already in the ring, his taped hands showing whitely even from here, his sloping, muscle-ridged back leaning forward on the stool.

The murmur and then the clap of hands and then the applause came down, and I loved it. They were only stringing with the champ until he was licked, but I loved it.

Through the ropes, and over to say hello to Patsy, and he just looked up and smiled his ring smile.

His handler was Pete Worden, and Pete came over to inspect the wrappings with Max. Then they went over to Patsy's corner together.

Charley said, "Luck, Luke," and Tony patted my shoulder and they went down below the apron.

I thought of Sally, back at the hotel. I wondered if she was worrying. Noodles had wanted to be here to see Patsy beat my brains out, but this one Noodles was missing. Or maybe not. Title fight and all, maybe They'd give him a three-day pass.

Across the ring, Patsy stared at me, smiling the fixed smile. Then Max blocked the image, as he kneaded the gloves and slipped them on. Max's sweat shirt was sour with sweat, and it was beaded on his forehead. A\dead cigar rolled in the corner of his mouth.

"Careful," he said hoarsely, "the early rounds. He's got the punch; he could be looking for a quickie. That low left he's going to show, that's a trap. Don't bite. You throw a right over it, he'll counterpunch you blind. Keep him in the open, this first round."

"Sure, sure, Max," I said. "We've talked it over a hundred times."

Jest rubbed the back of my neck, humming soothingly.

The introductions then, and going out for the instructions, and Gene Boyce was the third man. He said, "Title fight. You boys have had some dirty ones in your time, but you'd better keep this one clean, or I'll—"

Words, words, words, meaning nothing, but they like to sound important.

The house lights dimming; the arcs overhead coming into brilliant focus. *Now,* we go, we go, we go—

The bell.

I turned from the ropes, and Patsy was halfway across the ring, the left low, his feet flat, trying to catch me in a corner early.

Half-crouch, his big shoulders part of his armor, a hitter.

I feinted a right—and landed a clean, straight left alongside his nose.

It rained leather.

I hadn't fought a young man for a long time; I'd forgotten how fast and how hard they could hit. Patsy's hook came pounding in as he moved under my right hand. Three times it pounded me, twice in the midriff—and the third time in the groin.

I was backing toward the corner, and I could hear Max screaming "Foul" through the thunder of the fans. I brought my hands in and caught Patsy's nose with the laces and ripped.

He wanted it dirty; at my age, it would be better for me, but he wanted it dirty.

There was a throbbing in my groin, but it was a well-padded cup of ridged magnesium, and there'd been no permanent damage, yet.

Patsy was pounding at my kidney in the clinch and I managed a rabbit punch before Gene broke us.

Clean, Patsy broke, hands as high as any amateur's, putting on the red-blooded-American-boy act for the fans. They applauded his obvious sportsmanship.

I took one sideward step, and came in with the hook, bringing the swing of the body in with it. I tied him up and said, "I can play it either way, Patsy."

"Screw you, grandpa," he said.

I broke, missed him with a right, and caught him with the elbow, coming back. His mouthpiece went flying, and he stormed in.

Strong and young and dirty, fast and fit, he could punish. I rode with him, blocking what I could, draping my weight, keeping my hands and forearms in, watching his head. Downstairs, his hook tore at me, a big gun.

I tied him up, watching his head, his hard head. It could split a nose wide open, the way he'd learned to use it.

Blood dribbled down from his lower lip: I felt the sticky warmth of it on my shoulder.

Over Patsy's shoulder, I saw Max, and he was holding both hands aloft. Gene's hand smarted on my back.

Clean break, and I retreated. Patsy followed slowly, the heavy right cocked, the left higher now. I made our corner at the bell.

Gene was there when I flopped, and his face was flushed. "I told you guys *clean, clean, clean.* Stinking alley fighters."

"He started it, Gene," I said. "You saw the punch. I'll fight any way a man wants to fight. Don't try and tell me my business."

Max had his back to Gene, Jest had his eyes averted as he bathed my face. Max pulled my trunks out, felt for the cup, said over his shoulder, "We're busy, Gene."

Gene spun and went over to Patsy's corner.

Jest hummed. Max said, "You got the best of that. But watch that wop, watch him. You threw that hook off the step nice, nice."

"We go, we go," Jest said.

The buzzer, Max's "Careful," as they scrambled through the ropes. The bell.

Patsy came out slower than he had in the first round, and we met in ring center. He must have had some new advice; he circled away from my right hand, taking his time, his left shoulder guarding his chin. Somebody had told Patsy to be careful, too.

A quarter minute of that and some clown started to sing *The Blue Danube*. Someone shouted, "Your slip's showing."

Patsy came in.

He came into the straight left hand again, paused, and I tried a right for size.

It never landed. His own short and heavy right bounced off my chin, flashing from nowhere, and then his left pounded into my Adam's apple. For a moment I gagged and then moved in to clinch.

He stepped back and the first of three finishers caught me on the side of the face. It twisted my neck; the shock of it stopped my reason for a split second.

The second one was just above the button. The third one was the bull's-eye.

The arcs went shooting toward the stars and then erupted. For the first time in my career, I was headed for the canvas.

Chapter XIII

THE WIND ROARED, and the waves came pounding in at me on the rough, dry beach. Then the roar was a pulsation and the pulsation was a voice.

And the voice said, "Eight!"

New, rough canvas under my hands, and I scrambled desperately to get up. I was up at "nine," but Gene didn't come in to wipe the resin from my gloves; this ring was too new for resin.

I saw Patsy coming across toward me, and he seemed small, like the image in a reversed telescope. I retreated, and he moved faster. I saw the flash of his arm and pain screamed up from my groin.

I put my hands out and my right went around his neck. I lay on him, while he pounded the kidney with his right, while he tried to shove me off with the left.

I hung on, shaking the shadows from my brain, hoping some starch would come back to my legs. The ropes burned my back, the top of his head crashed my mouth, and then he had torn from my grasp.

The right I threw was blind, a desperation punch, knowing he was breaking so he could finish me. It was the luckiest right of my life. It caught him off balance.

Gene called it a knockdown, though it had been partly caused by Patsy's tangled feet. Gene picked up the count at "three" though Patsy was already up. At "eight," he waved him in.

I'd had those seconds, and I had the few more it took Patsy to get to my corner.

He came in slowly. He knew it had been a freak knock-down, but another freak poke could keep him from the title he'd cherished for years. He moved around me in a half-crouch.

The bell rang.

Ice at the back of the neck, smelling-salts, the wet, cold towel, Max's blunt fingers digging my legs into life. All this before a word.

And then the word was "Fool."

"I'll make it," I said. "I made that round. I'll make it."

"The first of the three," Max said, "an overhand right. What the hell is it, stigmatism?"

"I guess. Maybe a mental block. I'm all right, Max."

The buzzer, and Jest's massaging fingers left my neck, and Max sighed. I rose as the bell clanged, as Max shouted, *"Careful, now!"*

Patsy got to me before I made the center of the ring. I shoved the left out, as I had twice before and he automatically moved his head to his left.

As I brought over the right from the bleachers.

It caught him high, next to the eye, and he took a single, stumbling sideward, and I swarmed him.

But he was young, and he was strong. We traded hooks, and his had the steam. I tried a short right, and his was faster. I got on my bike.

The side of his face was red where I'd landed that round-opener; he had a puffed lower lip. But his eyes were bright and he hadn't lost an ounce of his moxie.

I kept the left in his eye, and had him missing for a full two minutes. Then he slid in under the left, bringing his hook with him.

Out of the three punches, two of them were low. I

wrestled him around until he tried to break—and then threw the top of my head into his nose.

The fans' screams were hysterical as he came back in, heeling me from mouth to forehead. I got in one solid blow under the heart before the bell.

Jest grinned. Max frowned. Max rinsed the mouthpiece, pulled out my trunks, sloshed me with water.

Max said, "Damned alley brawl."

Jest said, "We go, we go."

"To the nuthouse, we go," Max said. "To Queer Street."

"No more," Jest said. "This is the champ's, from here in. From this round on, it's going to be known as Mr. Pilgrim's progress. You'll see. We go."

How did he know? I knew, but I couldn't figure how he knew. That second round could happen to anybody, though it had never happened to me before. There'd be no more second rounds.

It got cleaner. Patsy slapped some, and tried a thumb a couple times, but the general tone of it was cleaner. He kept pounding me under the heart, every chance he got. I worked on the side of his face.

He was young and strong, but he was standard. There was no imagination in his strategy. I got the pattern of him, and began to score.

The left side of his face was beet-red now, from the right hands I'd parked there. The eye was puffing. I put more steam into my left hands to the face.

Max said, "You got him figured now."

"Right."

"Well, dump him."

"In time."

"Luke, that's not you talking."

"Some people are dead, Max." The buzzer.

"This won't bring 'em back."

"I'm quitting, after this one, Max. I don't want him in

the business after I quit. That much I owe the boys."

"Luke, that's—" The bell.

A real stiff one I parked under the heart, and his chin went back and his Adam's apple was a target I could reach.

His eyes watered; he gasped, clawing for breath. I smashed his open mouth, and retreated.

"Now, now, now—" the fans chanted. "Now, now, now—"

Not now.

On my stool, and Max said nothing to me. From below, Tony said, "You're looking better, Champ," and I nodded.

To the left of Patsy's feet, Paul D'Amico's bald head glistened and Paul D'Amico's cold eyes glared. I smiled at him.

He went down three times in the eighth round, twice more in the ninth. If Dutch had been in his corner, the towel would be in the ring now. But D'Amico could hope for a miracle.

And why didn't Gene stop it? Maybe Gene wanted to clean up the business a little, too.

Max said, "This Luke Pilgrim I don't know, and I don't want to know."

"He knows what he's doing," Jest said. "Leave the champ alone, Max."

In Patsy's corner, the doc said he was able to continue. He looked at D'Amico as he said it.

The bell.

"Now, now, now," the fans chanted, and they were right.

I hit him under the heart three times, and he stood wavering on his rubber legs.

I threw the hardest right hand I'd ever thrown in my life and caught him dead center.

There wasn't any need to count. Gene picked it up at "three" and went through the arm-swinging ritual, came over to lift my hand high and make the announcement, and Patsy was still out.

They were quiet, in the dressing-room, the reporters. They asked their questions and left. Some friends came in, the ones who may have guessed what I'd been trying to do, but even they didn't have many words.

Jest smiled and hummed, and Max changed his clothes.

"Maybe it'll be all right tomorrow," Max said. "Maybe I'll understand. Tonight, I'm going to get drunk." He left.

Tony said, "Charley and I got a couple broads lined up, Luke. See you later."

Only Jest was left. He asked, "You going home, Champ, or you going to celebrate?"

"I've got a date with some people. Business, Jest. I'll see you tomorrow." .

"Right. You looked good. You looked awful good to-night."

"Not to Max."

"Max is soft. But he'll understand."

"I hope. Good night, Jest."

"Night, Champ."

The door closed behind him, and I was alone. I heard his leather heels clacking on the concrete of the corridor, outside, getting dimmer and dimmer.

I heard the thump, thump, thump of my heart and watched the drop of sweat rolling off my hand. I was showered and dressed, I was ready to go, but I stood there for seconds.

I went over the words in my mind, the kind of words a man like D'Amico might listen to after the financial licking he must have taken.

Then I went out into the clear, cold night, the keys to the rented car jangling in my hand. I was colder than the night should make me; I guess I was scared.

I took Sepulveda down, the winding road through the

hills, like open country, like there wasn't a city for miles. I took it all the way to Venice Boulevard and then cut toward the ocean.

I was still the middleweight champion of the world; no gun with any brains was going to get involved in a murder that headline-worthy. The crown was my shield. Unless D'Amico had gone off his nut. I remembered the way he'd glared at me from ringside.

Here was Lincoln Boulevard and I turned and drove a couple blocks, and here was *Harry's Hoot Owl Club*.

There was a Caddy in the parking-lot and a Buick Special. There was a bleached and battered station wagon. Tony Scarpa sat behind the wheel, smoking a cigarette.

"Call Sally," I told him. "Tell her I'm all right. Tell her I won and I'm retiring. And tell her I love her."

"Or *loved* her," Tony said nervously. "Do you know what you're doing, Luke?" His cigarette was a small meteor, arching toward the driveway.

"I think I do. They don't kill guys my size."

"You'd like to believe. Want me along?"

"No. It's not your baby, Tony. Thanks a lot. I'll look you up tomorrow."

The station wagon went away, and I went up the dark steps to the dark doorway. A man stood there.

Charley Retzer.

"You remembered, huh, Luke? Your memory came back. She talked about me, huh?"

"I don't remember any of it, Charley."

"Well, how do you know, then? How did you learn I killed her? D'Amico? He didn't *know*. Noodles, but he—"

"Let's go in, Charley," I said.

There was a *Closed* sign on the door, but a light showed through the Venetian blinds of the window. I turned the knob, and the door was open, and we went in.

Harry was behind the bar; D'Amico and Johnny were

on stools in front of the bar.

Harry said, "Lock the door, Charley."

I heard the door click behind me. I went over and took one of the stools. I said, "Whisky, Harry. I won't need to train any more."

"You quitting, Champ?"

"I don't know. But I won't need to train."

D'Amico said, "You've got a lot of guts, Pilgrim."

"I need them in my business," I said. "Drop much, Paul?"

"I probably dropped more than you ever made, Pilgrim."

"Did I promise to dive? Did you have any reason to make that kind of an investment without preliminary planning?"

Silence from him. Then, finally: "What's on your mind?"

"Murder, and using me for a stooge. Manipulating me. I'm probably not very important, but the title is, and the title-holder shouldn't have to be anybody's stooge."

"A lot of 'em have been."

"Not this one."

Charley said, "When are you going to get to me? What about me?"

I said, "Ask Harry."

He turned to Harry. "You squealed?"

The big man shook his head. "Luke just guessed. He found out Bevilaqua means 'drink water' and he added it up from there. Right, Champ?"

"Right. That was the name of the doctor who ran that small hospital. Your brother, Harry?"

"Cousin."

"So what," Charley asked. "That's a case?"

"I haven't a case. I'm not a cop. But everything else adds. The doctor had to mention the time when he called us, in order to establish your alibi. He had to mention you were picked up at eleven, when Brenda had died after midnight. You were looking for me. Why? Because you were afraid of what she might have told me about you being her boy friend. You were the missing guy at Sam Wald's party, one of the principals in the fight. Sulking, Charley? And then after the trimming I gave you, you see me leave her apartment. Is that the way it was?"

"It's a good guess, I suppose. It makes a good story."

Behind me, Harry coughed. On his stool, D'Amico watched me. Johnny stared at the floor. I downed the whisky.

I said, "When we saw you in the hospital, even your hands were under the blankets. It was too hot a day for that. But you left some flesh from one hand on Brenda's teeth. The cops have the scrapings, Charley."

"You're still guessing."

"I am. There was a windmill sign near that hospital and another near Brenda's apartment. So my unconscious mind knows and it's trying to tell me. Some day it will cough it up. But I still won't be a cop, Charley."

"Windmill signs? What kind of sense does that make?"

"None to you, Charley." I turned to Harry. "You worry about Noodles. *You* killed Noodles."

On his stool, Johnny stirred.

Harry said, "Easy, Champ. I got a lot of bottles here."

"You didn't poison him," I went on, "but you killed him. You knew Charley had killed Brenda. If you'd gone to the law with it, Noodles would never have died."

"Charley's my friend," he said, "and I don't know that he killed anybody." His voice shook slightly.

"You know. You're damned sure in your own mind. Did he phone here, after he killed her? Did Noodles pick him up, too, and take him to that sanitarium or hospital, or what the hell it was?"

"I don't know what you're talking about," Harry said.

"All right. Charley doesn't, either." I took a flyer. "But I already remember the maroon silk sheets. Maybe the rest will come."

"You son-of-a-bitch," Charley said. "You—"

D'Amico said, "Easy, Charley."

Charley turned to Harry. "Whisky."

"Have they had you scared since you fought Giani? Have they had you scared all that time, Charley?" I asked him.

D'Amico said, "You've used a lot of words but none of them mean much to me. Scarpa said you were willing to talk business."

Behind me Harry said, "What the hell?"

"Maybe I do want to talk business," I told D'Amico. "But not as a stooge, Paul. Maybe a partner, but no stooge."

"A partner? What are you bringing into the partnership?"

"The title. That's why Max isn't here."

"You mean you're looking for new management?"

"No. Another fight with Patsy. This time, I bet along with you. My money rides with yours. That safe enough?"

He took a deep breath. "It would take a long time to get back the money I lost tonight. What else did you have in mind? Why all this business about Charley?"

"Because we want a killer," I said. "We want somebody for the law."

"We? Who's 'we'?"

"Harry and I. Tell him who we want, Harry. And pour me another drink."

Harry poured the drink, then looked up, and over at Johnny.

D'Amico's eyes followed the gaze. D'Amico looked at Johnny, back at Harry, then at me. "Are you crazy?"

"He killed Noodles," I said. "Noodles was Harry's friend. He's a killer, and you don't need him any more, Paul. You've outgrown the need for a man like that."

Johnny was motionless, standing where he could face all of us, his eyes steady on D'Amico, like a dog's eyes on his master.

"Insane," D'Amico said quietly. "You're crazy."

"You're big league, now," I said. "A lawyer is your gun. Johnny's a hang-over from the prohibition days. He's as dead as the dodo. If the law doesn't get him, I think maybe Harry will, some day. The state does it cleaner."

Johnny's eyes moved from D'Amico to Harry and back to his master. I think he wanted to talk. His mouth opened and closed.

"What have you got against him?" D'Amico said. "That business in the hotel with your girl, when you thought he was blocking the door? Is that it? Or are you nuts?"

"Maybe I'm nuts," I said. "I came here to do business. I don't want him in any business of mine. I guess you do. I guess you're still selling cut whisky to cheap night clubs, Paul." I finished my second drink. "Well, no dice?"

"We can do business," he said. "Don't rush off. I'll never turn him over to the law, but I can pension him, if he bothers you. I like Johnny, but I don't have to have him around."

Johnny's eyes flared, and his right hand jerked.

D'Amico caught it. He said, "Watch it, Johnny. You're not shooting anybody here, not yet."

Johnny's hand continued, and the gun came out. It wasn't pointing at anybody, but it was out. Looked like a .38, a revolver.

"Put it away, Johnny," D'Amico said. Quiet, his voice, but some tremor in it.

Johnny shook his head.

"Damn you," D'Amico said. "Put it away. These people

aren't punks, Johnny. Put that God-damned gun away!"

Johnny shook his head.

D'Amico stared at him. It must have been the first time in their association that Johnny had refused to obey an order.

Then D'Amico came off the stool, his hand out. "Give me that gun, you little bastard, or I'll—"

The gun turned, and now it was aimed at D'Amico, and D'Amico kept coming in on it.

I saw the flare and heard the smash of the shot. I saw D'Amico hurtle backward, and then saw the barrel of Johnny's gun swinging our way, and I hit the floor.

From the washroom, from a curtained booth, from a rear window, there were other guns, and shouts. I heard wood splinter, and then a *pang* and looked up to see the steel bar stool whirling, teetering, toppling—my way.

After the fight, I had to get knocked out.

Sally wore only shorts, no halter. "Am I brown?" she asked.

"You're fawn," I said. "You're a fawn, straight girl."

The sea below us, the sun above, a protected sundeck on this Malibu love nest; only I could see Sally. Only Sally and I, and she's seen herself before.

"Charley was jealous, then?" she asked.

"Mmmm. I don't know. He was battered and humiliated and half drunk, and probably saw me leave or enter his girl's place and maybe he was still scared of me. I don't know. He certainly wasn't scared of her."

"But this Johnny, turning on D'Amico like that."

"Johnny knew I loathed him. I'd called him a 'pimp.' I'd offered to rip his spine out. And then the boss wants to talk business with *me*. Temporary insanity, maybe?"

"Maybe. You couldn't plan on that, could you?"

"No. All I could plan on was that a whole platoon of

listening cops would get something they could use. I couldn't plan on Charley catching enough lead to make him think he was going to die, either. But that's why he confessed, and he might beat the rap. He's got the best lawyer in town, and he was almost out of his mind that night."

She turned over, giving me the front view. "And you still can't remember whether you did—whether you and Brenda were, or—"

"I can't remember a damned thing," I said. "That's the gospel, according to Luke."

She sniffed. "Maybe you can't even remember last night, huh? How about last night?"

"I'll never forget it, darling," I told her honestly. "I've been thinking of nothing else, all morning. Fellows always told me about it, but now I know it's true, and I'm glad."

"Fellows told you what? What's true?"

"It's just as much fun *after* you're married," I told her.

Printed in the United States
By Bookmasters